The Hellkeeper

Nova Black

The Hellkeeper

Copyright © 2025 Nova Black

All rights reserved.

No part of this book may be reproduced, stored in a retrieval system, or transmitted in any form or by any means — electronic, mechanical, photocopying, recording, or otherwise — without the prior written permission of the author, except in the case of brief quotations used in critical articles or reviews.

This is a work of fiction. All characters, names, events, places, and incidents are products of the author's imagination or are used fictitiously. Any resemblance to actual persons, living or dead, or real events is purely coincidental.

The name of the village mentioned in this book is entirely fictional. No such village exists, and any similarity to a real location is unintentional. It has been invented solely for storytelling purposes and is not meant to represent or offend any real place or community.

Nova Black asserts the moral right to be identified as the creator of this work.

First published in 2025

Cover design by [Raven Designs, https://ravencoverdesigns.co.uk/]

For information, inquiries, or permissions, please contact:

[authornovablack@proton.me]

Trigger Warnings

Nothing within these pages is meant to be glorified. This book contains themes that may be deeply disturbing or upsetting to some readers, including but not limited to: stalking, violence, torture, gun use, death, non-consensual and dubiously consensual situations, blasphemy, human sacrifice, cult-like environments, religious trauma, body mutilation, and extremely unhealthy, toxic dynamics. **Please proceed with caution as your mental health matters.**

Disclaimer

The religion, practices, and beliefs depicted in this book are entirely fictional and products of the author's imagination. They are not based on any real-world religion, culture, or spiritual tradition. No offense is intended toward any faith, belief system, or community. Similarly, the name of the village mentioned in this story is completely fictional. This book is written with love for all, and respect for every reader's beliefs and experiences.

Blurb

She ran from death straight into my arms.

She just doesn't know it yet.

I've been here from the start—watching, waiting, and breathing in the fear that clings to her skin. She prays to a god that doesn't listen, locks doors that don't keep me out, and walks through a world that I've already carved her name into. She thinks she's alone. She isn't.

I live in the shadows, in the walls, beneath her feet. I sleep under her bed. I steal the scent of her skin from the clothes she sets aside. I keep her safe, even as I pull the strings that unravel her sanity, thread by thread. She calls me a demon. A nightmare. *A Hellkeeper.*

She doesn't understand.

I didn't come to haunt her.

I came to claim her.

And when they try to take her from me, when they dare to rip her from my hands—I'll drag them to hell myself.

For the ones who dreamed of hands rough enough to shake the shame off.

… The Hellkeeper

Chapter One
Amelia

My meeting with the Hellkeeper is near, tomorrow at midnight, to be exact. Tomorrow at midnight, my blood will be spilled to please him. I will be sacrificed for the greater good, so my little village will be spared from fire, flames, and ash.

I'm not special. Not really. I haven't been chosen for my fair skin, my green eyes, or my dirty blonde hair. Just like the girls before me, whose fates remain a mystery after the sacrifice, I've been selected because I am of no use to this village.

I turned twenty-two a week ago, and the village now officially calls me a sphincter. I haven't secured a husband. I've always been too quiet, preferring to wander the woods, lost in my daydreams about a world far beyond this place instead of speaking with boys. With our tiny population, the competition for a partner is fierce, and I haven't helped my cause.

I have no husband to care for, no one who would miss me if I disappeared. I'm mediocre at best. I can't even fish properly; Bambi catches fish with her bare hands. Every time I was on cattle duty, a sheep or two would escape, courtesy of my constant daydreaming. But Neva and Meredith? The sheep practically obeyed them with just a glance. Seeds I planted in the dirt weren't necessarily blessed; most of the time, they didn't even grow.

I've never fit in here. Most of the girls got married at eighteen, trying to carry on the village's dying bloodline. But no one has had a baby that lived in over a decade—not since the last one, a girl, now fourteen. Miscarriages come like clockwork. The elders say it's because we aren't praying hard enough.

The girls my age think they're better than me because they can at least try. The younger ones still have a couple of years left before the village starts eyeing their wombs too. I can't offer anything. The boys say I'm not wife material. Too quiet. Too ordinary.

This place? It's cold. And dark. Always dark. Everyone walks around with that sense that something's about to go up in flames. You can feel it, like a hand around your throat.

No one cares if I'm gone. I'm invisible. The most forgettable, replaceable, and easily buried. The choice was easy.

My mother tucked me in for the last time, whispered goodbye in my ear, and steeled herself to leave me behind to face my fate. Even a mother's love cannot override the fear of him... the Hellkeeper. The one the scriptures have spoken of for a hundred years in Hell, Washington—population one hundred and fifty.

Our village is cursed, marked by misfortune and terror, and it's all because of the Hellkeeper. The stories warn that one day, if we displease him, he will set fire to everything. Nothing will survive. No crops. No life. Hell, Washington, will truly become a scorching red hell.

So, we sacrifice. We offer up one virgin girl every five years, just to stay in his good graces. The elders have sworn to uphold this tradition, anything to keep the village alive. Here, we pray ten times a day. We kneel until our knees are raw and our lips cracked from endless recitations. But if the village stays like this, they'll run out of girls to sacrifice in around thirty years, which is why the elders have taken to playing matchmaker as well as religious leaders.

No one really knows what the Hellkeeper is. The scripture never explains, just drops his name like we're supposed to understand. Is he a creature of light? Of darkness? Neither? Both? I've asked before, but no one has an answer. Some say he was once an angel, but something went wrong. Others think he was never anything close to human, never meant to be understood. He doesn't belong to heaven or hell. He just watches, waits. And when he comes, he never leaves empty-handed.

My heart always bled for the girls. They weren't much different from me. They were the black sheep, the forgotten ones. Most of them were orphans, with no one to mourn their absence. I watched them try so hard to fit in, to prove they were worth something. But they weren't fooling anyone, least of all me. The emptiness and deviance lurked within them; the same qualities I notice in myself when I stand in front of the mirror.

My mother sits outside my room, praying and praying and praying. But even she knows that no prayer will save me now.

I bury my face in the pillow, muffling my sobs. I'm trying to stay strong, but doubt creeps in through the cracks in my soul. Sleep comes, but it's anything but peaceful. I dream of fire engulfing the village, engulfing me. I dream of restraints closing in on me, paralyzing me. I dream of fear, pain, and smoke. I dream of a shadowy figure lingering under my bed, in my closet, in the walls…

I wake with a start. My beautiful mother is sound asleep beside me. Her gray hair doesn't diminish her beauty, but the wrinkles around her eyes have deepened in the last few days. The news of me being the chosen one has aged her prematurely. My father died when I was young, and when I'm ultimately sacrificed, she will have no one.

It's tomorrow now. The sky outside is pitch black, far past midnight. A sharp pang of desperation hits me when I realize I will never see the world beyond this place. I've spent my life dreaming about it, reading about it, wondering about it. The elders say there is nothing worth seeing, that everything beyond our borders is corruption waiting to seep into our bones. I used to believe them. But now? I wonder if they were just afraid.

If I don't do something for myself now, when will I? My life has been nothing but a series of meaningless tasks. I've lived in a loop of dreams that will never come true. Maybe I can achieve just one before this nightmare begins.

I've decided, selfishly, to run.

I untangle myself from my mother's arms as quietly as I can, my heart pounding in my chest. I slip into the kitchen, reach into the jar on the high shelf, and grab a few bills. It will hurt my mother's savings, but it's my dying wish.

My hair's a mess, my eyes are red from crying, and my lips are bleeding from the endless prayers. I'm wearing a loose white gown that covers my ankles, hiding all signs of womanhood. I'm too scared to make myself presentable. If I wake my mother, she'll stop me.

I slip on my sandals, tie back my tangled hair, and leave just as I am.

I crouch low, tiptoeing past the cottages. A drop of sweat falls from my forehead to my lips, the salty taste flooding my mouth.

Growing up here, you learn things no one ever says out loud. Like the fact that beyond the tree line, there's a set of tracks, and if you follow them long enough, they'll lead you to a station the village pretends doesn't exist. I just have to walk a little farther. And a little farther after that. Walk until I reach the train station miles away from the village.

When I finally reach a point where no more cottages are in sight, I run. The ground is muddy beneath my feet, sucking at my shoes with every step. The scent of wet leaves and damp earth clings to my skin as I push through the trees. The cold air stings my lungs, but all I feel is freedom. Real, raw freedom.

The only sound in the total darkness is the crunch of dead leaves under my shoes and my labored breaths. For the first time, I don't feel the weight of the village on my shoulders.

I feel alive.

Chapter Two
Amelia

I'm soaked to the bone by the time I get onto the train. My legs feel like they're going to fall off from the distance I walked, and the rain turned the dirt road into a muddy mess, staining my feet and the hem of my white dress. I wring the water out of my long hair and watch as it splatters onto the train floor.

I'm cold. I'm scared. But most of all...I'm alive.

The train is packed, even this late. Farmers heading home, their hands rough and their faces tired. Some glance at me with something like pity. Others sneer, their expressions twisting into something darker. Something hungry. I don't understand why. Do they know what I've done? That I've put my entire village at risk?

A voice crackles over the speakers. At first, I think the Hellkeeper is speaking to me from the sky, but no one else reacts. It's just an announcement.

The train slows, and a few men stand. One lingers. An old man with a limp and sun-worn skin. He quickly shrugs off his jacket and puts it in my lap.

"Stay safe, girl," he croaks out.

He doesn't wait for a thank you, just shuffles off the train. I blink down at the jacket, pressing the warm fabric against me. The elders always said the outside world was cruel, but that man just gave me the only thing keeping him warm. What else have they lied about?

The train jerks to a stop.

"Downtown," the voice announces.

I step off, shaking the weight of those men's eyes off my shoulders. The city is loud. The air is sharp and chemical, nothing like the clean, open fields back home. Lights pulse everywhere, flashing, glowing, unnatural.

A horn blares, and I nearly leap out of my skin as a man leans out of a car window, cursing at me. People around me don't react. They just stand there, waiting, and I stand close to them. A woman steps toward me, rummaging through her bag before holding out a few bills.

People just give money away here? But her eyes are not kind. She's staring at my too-big jacket, my muddy feet, my stained dress. Her lips purse. She waves the money at me again, rolling her eyes this time, as if this is some grand favor.

It doesn't feel right.

I push her hand away gently. "No, thank you."

She huffs, shoving the bills back into her bag before turning her back to me. Weird.

The little figure on the post turns green. The people move. I follow.

I wander past towering buildings that stretch so high my neck aches to look at them. How can something like this exist? Humans built this? It's too grand, too impossible.

But I don't stop. If this is my first and last day of freedom, I won't spend it staring.

Food stalls line the street, the smell of hot oil and grilled meat wrapping around me, making my stomach twist painfully. I hesitate. I have a little money left, but I need it for the train ride home. Still… if not now, when? Hell doesn't have street vendors, I'm sure of it.

I buy a hotdog on a stick. When I hand the vendor my money, he frowns, then sighs and hands some of it back. Right. I'm bad at this. We rarely used money in the village. I don't know what things are worth.

Sadness creeps in.

I'll never get to learn.

Further down, a glowing machine catches my eye, stuffed with plush toys. A boy, maybe a few years older than me, steps up to it. He slides a bill in, moves a little joystick, and a claw drops down, grabbing a red plushie. He wins on his first try.

Excitement sparks in my chest.

My turn.

I feed a bill into the slot. The machine hums to life. My hands tremble as I maneuver the claw over a teddy bear and press the button. The claw drops. Misses.

I try again. And again. And again.

Just one more try. Just one more.

Finally, the claw grips the bear and drags it to the chute. A victorious jingle plays. I snatch the bear up, pressing it to my chest.

And then I freeze.

I turn to my palm.

Empty.

I check my pockets. My heart slams against my ribs. My money's gone.

Gone.

I used the last of it on this stupid bear.

Panic crashes over me, cold and suffocating. No train ride home. No way back to the village. No way back at all.

The sky rumbles.

A second later, rain pours, thick and heavy, soaking through my clothes in seconds. My hair sticks to my face. My body shakes violently from the cold.

I walk. I don't know where I'm going. My vision blurs. My legs weaken. My breaths shorten.

Then—

Black.

***

I force my eyes open when I feel a presence by my side. An old woman stands over me, and she looks heavily concerned.

"Are you okay?" she asks.

I open my mouth, but nothing comes out.

"You're shaking. Come, let's get you inside."

She helps me sit up. I glance around. We're outside a small restaurant, its lights dimmed. She must own it.

"Do you have somewhere to go?"

Where do I have to go? Back to the village that wants to sacrifice me to the Hellkeeper? Or to these streets, where I'll starve and freeze? So, I don't answer. I truly don't know what to say.

"Are you in trouble?" She whispers

I nod.

She glances around warily before making a decision. "Come inside."

"You don't have to tell me anything. Just get out of the cold." She quickly adds when she notices how hesitant I am.

I follow her in, and she drapes a blanket around me. I grip it like a lifeline, thankful for the warmth.

"There now," she sighs as she wraps another blanket around my shivering form. "What's your name, dear?"

"Amelia," I manage to croak out.

"Well, Amelia, I'm Margret," she tells me. "Sit down. I'll make you some tea."

I obey without thinking, my legs weak beneath me. The restaurant is small but very cozy. It reminds me of back home. A handwritten menu board hangs above the counter. It still smells like the dishes she made throughout the day, but right now, all I care about is the tea she's making.

She hands me the cup before sitting next to me. "Do you feel comfortable telling me what's wrong now?"

My grip on the tea mug turns white-knuckled as I fight back my panic. If I tell her the truth she'd think I'm insane. She'd send me right back out into the night.

But it spills out of me anyway.

"The village," I whisper, my voice barely carrying over the rain outside. "The one I came from. They're going to sacrifice me soon."

Her face goes pale. The kind of pale that drains the blood straight from her skin. Her lips part slightly before she presses them together, as if she's holding back a reaction.

She swallows. "What village?"

"Hell."

She recoils like I just spit in her face. I brace myself for her to mock me, even kick me out.

"I always knew," she murmurs, half to herself. "That village—there were rumors. Dark ones. But rumors aren't enough to make the police listen."

The Hellkeeper

"You believe me?" I ask, perplexed, my eyes as wide as saucers. We've always been told that the city doesn't believe in anything spiritual.

She nods, and validation floods my system.

"How can I help?" she asks.

The question makes me shrink into myself. Shame burns in my chest because I know what I need, but I don't want to ask. I'm no beggar. I'm not someone who takes advantage of kindness. But what else can I do?

"Could you...could you give me enough for the train back home?" I say, even though it's the last thing I want. She's already done enough. I shouldn't have asked.

She shakes her head, and I push back from the chair, guilt and humiliation tangling inside me. "I'm sorry. I shouldn't have—"

Before I can leave, she pulls me back to the chair gently.

"Do you want to be sacrificed?" she asks tentatively, but she already knows the answer. Maybe she just asked to make me realize it.

Yet, the question still stuns me. The answer is obvious. No. No, I want to live. But saying it feels like admitting something very selfish. What would come of the village? Who else would they choose?

I don't want to die, but what other choice do I have? Run and starve on the streets? Stay and let the Hellkeeper take me? There may be a way out; the ritual says only virgins can be sacrificed. If I lose that, they won't offer me to him. They'll just kill me instead. So, it's not even a solution in the first place.

"No," I whisper. It feels like I've admitted a huge sin. The elders would have slapped me straight across the face.

She watches me for a long moment before she speaks. "Then stay here."

"What?" It feels like the earth stopped spinning.

"I could use an extra pair of hands around here. And there's a bed in the storage room. I sleep there sometimes when I get too tired during shifts. You can have it."

I can't process what she's saying. She's offering me safety, a place to stay, work.

There may really be a way out.

Chapter Three
Damien

Fuck.

I raise my pistol again and pull the trigger. The man chasing me doesn't even get the chance to scream before the bullet rips through his skull. He drops, blood pooling beneath him like a crimson halo.

One down. Three left.

I keep moving. Fast.

When I got the order to eliminate James Brown—the king of child porn distribution—I expected some outrage. But not this. Not ten fucking men tailing me like I'm some cornered prey.

Too bad for them. I don't get hunted.

I am the hunter.

A bullet slices past my cheek, close enough to burn. I pivot, raising my pistol and squeezing the trigger. It should be another clean kill, another body to drop, but nothing happens.

Click.

Empty.

Fuck.

I push harder, my muscles burning as I take off down the alley. Hiding isn't my style, but without bullets, I don't have a choice. My boots hit the pavement loudly as I scan for cover. My eyes lock onto a small restaurant at the corner of the street. It's dark, closed, and empty.

Perfect.

I round the building, crouching low. The back door is unlocked. *Tsk*. I'm amused at the sheer stupidity. A mistake like this gets people killed. But tonight, it's saving my ass.

I slip inside, as quiet as a ghost. The restaurant is small; just a couple of wooden tables pushed against the walls, a tiny spotless kitchen, and air thick with the scent of old grease and stale coffee.

I sink into a chair, muscles coiled tight, grip still firm around the empty pistol. A habit. Through the tinted windows, I watch them sprint past, guns raised like they expect me to pop out and make their job easier.

They lost me.

No one would be this pissed over James Brown's death unless they were just like him; filthy, disgusting predators. The kind of men who deserve a bullet between the eyes. The kind of men I've spent my life hunting down.

I lean my head back against the chair. I should get up and leave now that my trail has gone cold.

But something tugs at me. That deep, primal instinct I never ignore.

Get up. Look. Hunt.

I push to my feet and start moving. The restaurant is dark and silent, but something calls me deeper.

My boots barely make a sound as I stalk across the floor, down a narrow hall, past the kitchen, toward stairs leading down.

Logic says, Turn around. Get the hell out. But the voice pulling me to investigate is louder than logic.

I move down the steps. The air shifts as I reach the bottom; it's colder, heavier. There's a door at the end, cracked open. Dim light spills through the gap, stretching toward me like a hand trying to pull me in.

I step closer, and I see her.

Lying on a bed, wrapped in blankets, deep in sleep.

An angel.

There's no other word for it. She looks like she was put here by mistake; something divine trapped in a world full of filth. I've never seen anyone so perfect in my thirty years on this earth. Her hair spills over the pillow in waves. She's flawless and delicate in a way that makes something violent stir inside me.

Her chest rises and falls with every breath. Adorable little snores escape her.

I just stand there. Watching.

What the fuck is she doing here?

And why do I feel like I was meant to find her?

She doesn't belong here.

Not in this rotting excuse for a bed. Not in a fucking storage room that smells of damp wood. Not wrapped in a blanket rough against skin that should only know silk and lace.

A girl like her should be in the finest penthouses, where monthly rent costs more than most people make in a year. She should have people falling at her feet, desperate for just a second of her attention. She should be covered in diamonds.

Instead, she's here. Forgotten. Vulnerable. Mine.

The light above her illuminates her doll-like features. She's ethereal, like a being put on this earth just to test men like me.

I could swear she glows from the inside, like something holy.

She doesn't turn the lights off to sleep.

Is she scared of the dark?

She has every right to be. Because tonight, a monster crawled out of it and basked in her innocence.

I kneel beside the bed, close enough to feel the warmth she emits. My fingers itch to touch, to take, to claim. She's so small. So soft.

I barely brush my knuckles against her cheek, and the heat that sparks up my arm is enough to make me repent. Something deep inside me snaps like a cord pulled too tight.

I do it again, drag my fingers across the line of her jaw, down the column of her throat.

She stirs, shifting slightly. I twist a strand of her hair around my palm, bring it to my face, and rub it along my jaw, my lips. I could drown in her scent. I could fucking die in this moment and be happy. I let the strand slip from my fingers, watching as it falls back across her pillow like spun gold.

My fingers twitch. Fighting the urge to bury themselves in it. To fist it. To pull. To mark.

My lips part, breath ragged. I lean in to press my nose against her temple, breathe her in, and my eyes roll back at the scent of her.

Something sweet. Something innocent. Something pure.

I could stay here forever.

Watching. Waiting. Guarding.

No.

Not just guarding.

Owning.

She needs me.

She has no idea, but she does.

If she's here, sleeping in a goddamn storage room, then she has no one. No family. No friends. No one to protect her from the world.

No one but me.

I'll give her everything.

A life fit for a queen.

I'll worship her. Ruin her. Corrupt her until there's no part of her left untouched by me.

She'll wake up wrapped in silk. In gold. In my arms.

She just has to accept it.

Even leaving her now seems impossible.

I swallow hard, possessiveness clawing at my throat.

No. I won't leave. Instead, I crouch down, pressing my hands to the cold floor, and slide under the bed. The wood creaks at my weight, but she doesn't wake. The curve of her arm dangles over the edge, close enough to touch.

I clench my fists to stop myself.

I close my eyes.

And I wait.

Chapter Four
Amelia

It's been a week.

A week since I walked away from my village. A week since I chose myself over them. It was a selfish decision, but I just can't bring myself to regret it.

But that also means it's been a week since someone else took my place. There's no way the ritual stopped just because I ran. They must have chosen another girl.

The thought curls around my throat like it's going to choke me from the inside out, but I shove it down. Guilt won't bring her back, whoever she was. Whoever they decided was next.

My hands press into the dough, fingers kneading, pushing, stretching. Margaret works alongside me, seasoning some chicken breasts. Her presence is warm. She doesn't hover or scold me when I make mistakes. She lets me learn at my own pace.

Not like them.

Not like the village where every mistake I ever made was broadcast and shamed. Margaret isn't like that. She's been nothing but kind. Accepting.

Guilt rears its ugly head again. I left them behind. And because of that, someone else was sacrificed. *No*.

Stop. I can't think like that. I had to leave. I had to. What was I supposed to do? Offer myself to the monster that has terrorized my village for years?

My fingers dig too hard into the dough, and Margaret hums at me, as if telling me to get out of my own head. I let out a breath, easing my grip, smoothing the surface again.

The restaurant has changed since I started working here. The air isn't as stale. The tables don't wobble like they used to; courtesy of me tightening the screws. The menu is wider, with some dishes from back home. It's cleaner, fresher.

Better, if I may say so myself.

Margaret told me yesterday that before I came along, she barely got a customer or two. That people passed this place by without a second glance, but now, business is picking up. I don't know why that makes something warm settle in my chest. I shouldn't feel like I belong here. Not yet. Maybe not ever.

The bell above the door chimes. A man walks in, and I immediately move to serve him. He makes his way to a table without looking at his path once, his eyes glued to the small glowing square in his hand. A smartphone. I only recently learned what they were called. My little village is so behind on these inventions, it should be illegal.

He smacks his gum loudly, making my skin crawl. It doesn't get better when he finally speaks; he still doesn't even glance my way.

"Yeah, uh... burger. No pickles. Fries. Coke." He snaps his fingers at me. "And hurry it up."

"Of course, sir."

He doesn't acknowledge me. Just keeps tapping at his phone. I glimpse Margaret watching from behind the counter with a frown.

I rush to prepare the order, making sure everything is exactly as he asked. I double-check. Triple-check. Finally, I carry the tray to his table.

"Enjoy," I say softly as I set his food down.

For the first time, he actually looks at me, but he glares like I'm an annoying fly that won't stop buzzing in his ear.

"Are you fucking kidding me?"

"Sir?"

He shoves the plate forward, knocking over his drink. "I said no pickles."

I stare at the burger, certain I didn't put pickles in it. I know because I checked. Twice.

"I—I'm sure I—"

I flinch as he slams his hands on the table.

"Jesus Christ, just fucking fix it."

What can I say? He's not even letting me explain. My hands shake at my sides. I don't want to argue with him, the customer is always right, after all.

All I can do is nod quickly and reach for the plate, but he's already standing. He doesn't even give me a chance to "fix" this. He storms out, cursing me under his breath.

This is humiliating. It feels like ropes are wrapping around my lungs. I can't breathe.

What if Margaret kicks me out?

What if I messed up?

What if—

A warm hand touches my shoulder.

It's Margaret, and she looks at me with sympathy.

"Don't," she says gently. "Don't let an ass like that get to you."

She rubs slow circles into my back. I don't think she even realizes she's doing it, but it fills me with relief; she's not mad at me.

With a huff, she pulls a small envelope from her apron pocket and holds it out to me.

"What's this?"

"Your pay for the week."

I shake my head fast. "No, Margaret." I take a step back. "I don't need it. You've already done more than enough."

"What you need is to go buy yourself something nice." She presses the envelope into my palm. "And take the day off. I've got it from here."

"But—"

"No 'but.'" She folds my fingers over the money. "Go."

I should insist. Truly, I will never be able to repay her, even if I work in the restaurant for free for years. But what I've learned about Margaret over the past week is that she's very stubborn. So, I agree.

***

I roam the streets carefully, dodging shoulders, watching the way everyone moves with such purpose. I don't know if I'll ever walk like that.

A shop catches my eye, it's a boutique with a mannequin in the window dressed in something that makes you want to spin in front of a mirror. I walk in, trailing my fingers down different dresses, but one in particular catches my eye.

The color is a deep, emerald green and it feels like silk. The neckline dips just enough to feel like a secret. The skirt is full, made to catch a breeze. I lift it off the rack, pressing it against me. It's perfect. Then I check the price tag.

My stomach drops.

I put it back immediately. Ever since I started working at the restaurant, I've become smarter with money. I may still have a lot to learn, but one thing I'm sure of is that this dress is worth more than a week's revenue at the restaurant. Much more.

I shake it off and leave.

Outside, the cold air stings my face. The city feels louder now, harsher.

A small shape is curled up by a building; a cat. Thin. Patchy fur. Trembling. It flinches away from people as if expecting to be kicked.

I turn and step into a convenience store without a second thought. Five minutes later, I crouch in front of the cat, peeling open a can of tuna. It stares at me, suspicious. But hunger wins out. It slinks closer, sniffing before taking the first bite.

"There you go," I murmur. "Better than nothing, right?"

Eventually, the cat finishes and licks its paws, already forgetting I exist. Typical.

The sun bleeds into the horizon, deep oranges fading into bruised purples. By the time I reach the restaurant, the windows are dark. Margaret's already locked up for the night.

I fish my key from my pocket, hands stiff from the cold, and slip inside. The restaurant's atmosphere has become comforting. Familiar. I lock the door behind me and make my way to the back.

The storage room is small, but it's mine. A bed is shoved against the wall, and a small bedside drawer houses all my belongings, which are not much. The lamp flickers as I turn it on, casting everything in a dim glow.

My eyes widen when I notice something on my bed. It's the emerald green dress from the store, it's lying there, spread out like something waiting for me. My heart stutters.

There's a box beside it. A gift box.

The box is smeared with something dark, something that looks too much like blood.

My ears ring.

My hands shake as I undo the lid. Inside, nestled in white tissue paper, is a severed human tongue.

The air leaves my lungs. A sharp, choked sound gets caught in my throat.

My vision blurs, my body locking up, refusing to process what's in front of me.

There's a note.

The paper is folded neatly, placed right beside the tongue. I force my fingers to unfold it.

The words are scrawled in deep, jagged ink.

No one disrespects my angel and walks away unscathed. Now, be good and put on the dress for me.

I drop the note. The room tilts, my breaths coming too fast, too shallow.

There's something wrong in the air.

Something watching.

I am not alone.

Chapter Five
Damien

They say obsession is a drug. I wouldn't know. I never needed narcotics, never indulged in anything that could cloud my judgment. Weak men use substances to escape their reality. I have always welcomed the darkness, the pain, the hunt.

But this?

This is unlike anything I have ever known.

It's worse than any addiction, deeper than any craving. It's in my blood now, pumping through me every second of the day. It poisons me in the most exquisite fucking way.

Her.

Amelia.

My angel.

She's hiding under her blanket as if that could protect her, as if it could keep her safe from the monster lurking just beneath her bed.

Me.

Her breathing is laced with terror.

Poor thing.

My gift scared the shit out of her.

I didn't mean for that. Well, maybe a little. She needs to understand and know that she isn't meant to be treated like trash by men who don't even deserve to look at her.

That's why I had to kill him.

I saw the way he spoke to her. The way his face twisted in disgust. How he slammed his hand against the table like she was some dog meant to cower at his feet.

I wanted to break him right then and there. But he didn't deserve a quick death.

So I followed him.

Dragged him into the shadows and made sure he understood what it meant to disrespect her. What it meant to make her cry.

He begged.

He screamed.

He choked on his own fucking blood.

And when I took the knife and sliced out that useless tongue of his, I thought of her. I thought of how soft her voice is, how she stutters when she's unsure, how she tries so hard to please, even when people don't deserve it.

He didn't deserve her words.

Didn't deserve to speak to her.

So I made sure he never would again.

And now, she's here. My beautiful girl, so terrified she won't let her hands or feet dangle over the side of the bed. As if a monster might snatch them up.

Leaving her at night is impossible. I tried. Walked three blocks before something inside me snapped. I turned around like a fucking rabid dog, crawling back to her.

She needs me.

She just doesn't know it yet.

I don't sleep; not really. Not when she's this close. Instead, I listen. To her breath. To the occasional soft whimper she lets out. Sometimes, she mutters words I don't understand, the sound like extravagant prayers. I want to know everything that goes on in her mind. I want to dismantle her. Instead, I settle for reaching out from under the bed to grasp the end of the blanket. Just enough to feel closer to her.

She belongs to me now.

And very soon, she will know it. Worship it.

My angel will crawl to me in the darkness, in the trenches, and play with her monster. Her devil.

Fuck.

The vibration in my pocket rips me from my trance, from the sick pleasure of being this close to her.

A job.

Another hit.

I clench my jaw, inhaling slow and deep. Sheer fucking rage bubbles up at the thought of leaving her alone.

If I didn't have a reputation to uphold, I'd be up her ass twenty-four seven.

I crawl out from under the bed, not caring to be quiet; she already knows I'm here. I stretch out my limbs, shaking off the stiffness in my muscles.

She's trembling. Shaking like a leaf caught in a storm.

A faint whisper escapes her lips, and I still. What is she saying?

I take a step closer, then another, leaning in just enough to hear the soft, hurried words spilling from her mouth. She's praying.

Her voice is raw, desperate; each word more fervent than the last. It spills from her lips like poetry spun in agony.

I close my eyes, letting the sound wash over me.

I almost laugh.

 Almost.

Nothing can save her from me. Even in hell, I would seek her out.

I pull the bloody gift box off her bedside drawer, slipping it into my pocket. She'll freak the fuck out if it's still here in the morning, and I don't want her losing more sleep than she already will.

Something gnaws at me. It stops me from leaving. A temptation that consumes me alive, swallowing me whole.

So I listen.

I step back to the bed, standing right beside her.

Her prayers increase, faster, louder, as if she can feel me, as if some instinctual part of her knows I'm right here, watching, breathing her in. The scent of her fills my lungs, and my eyes roll back. Slowly, I press a kiss to her head through the blanket, letting my lips linger on the woman I've claimed.

She screams bloody murder, hiding further under the blanket. With a sigh, I straighten. She's not ready yet. But she will be. She will get used to me.

I turn and walk out, her frantic prayers chasing after me.

***

Oliver Miller. Clean-cut. Polite. The kind of guy mothers trust and women let their guard down around. But he's a monster under the badge. A serial rapist.

This time, he picked the wrong girl. Her father is in the Mob, and the second he found out, Oliver's fate was sealed. A dead man walking.

He doesn't even get the chance to scream. I carve the blade straight through his throat, severing muscle and bone. His body twitches violently, eyes wide and haunted. Blood surges from his neck, soaking his police uniform.

I crouch down and grip his hair. His head separates from his shoulders. The request was clear: They wanted his head. So I deliver.

Knives aren't my favorite tool of elimination, but when the client wants it, I oblige.

I wrap it up, stuff it into a duffel bag, and wipe my blade on his shirt. Gore doesn't bother me. Nothing does.

***

The meeting spot is an upscale cigar lounge. The kind of place where men like Richard Davis sit in luxury while dealing in blood. He's already waiting for me, a thick cigar smoldering between his fingers. His daughter, Linda, sits beside him, her eyes locked on me like I just descended from the heavens.

I drop the bag onto the table. Blood seeps through the fabric, staining everything it touches. The stench of death is heavy, mixing with the scent of tobacco and overpriced cologne.

Richard takes a drag of his cigar. "You always deliver, Damien."

I say nothing. It is expected of me to be the best at what I do.

He pulls the bag open just enough to peek inside. A grin stretches across his face. "Perfect," he murmurs, zipping it back up. "You do fine work. My daughter got her justice."

Linda leans forward, her eyes shimmering with something sickly sweet. "You're incredible," she breathes. "My savior."

I grunt in response, barely sparing her a glance.

Richard chuckles. "Efficient and humble. A rare breed." He pulls out a big black bag and hands it to me. Payment. I take it without counting. His money is always good.

Linda is still staring at me, waiting for something. A smile, a thank you, anything.

She won't get it.

My gaze drops to the diamonds dripping from her ears, her throat, her wrists. Everywhere her skin is exposed, she's draped in wealth.

Expensive. Luxurious.

A man like Richard dresses his daughter in status. Makes sure everyone knows she is his.

My girl doesn't own diamonds.

Unacceptable.

Chapter Six
Amelia

Fear coils in my stomach, corroding my insides like acid. It slithers up my throat, burning my flesh from the inside out. I'm not losing my mind. I can't be.

But something—someone—was under my bed last night. I know it. I felt it.

God. The memories are branded behind my eyelids, etched into my mind forever. The gift box. The blood. The tongue. The note.

No one disrespects my angel.

I swallow down bile.

The Hellkeeper. It has to be him. That makes sense, doesn't it? I was meant to die, but I ran. Maybe this is his way of reminding me. Of toying with me before he finally drags me under.

My knees wobble. I clutch the counter for balance. I can't think about this now. I can't. I have orders to take, tables to wipe, dishes to clean. If I stop, if I let myself spiral, I won't be able to climb back up.

So I work. I take orders and force smiles, staying busy. It helps. A little.

Until a voice makes me jump so hard I nearly drop a plate.

"Jesus, girl, you're skittish today." Margaret chuckles, wrinkled eyes crinkling in amusement. "What, a monster sneak up on you?"

"Guess I'm just on edge."

Margaret hums, unconvinced, and steps forward. I tense. She watches me closely. I focus on stirring the pasta, trying to avoid her gaze. Her hand reaches up and brushes against my neck.

She lifts the necklace between her fingers, letting the diamonds catch the dim kitchen light. It looks ridiculous against my polyester uniform.

"You got this yesterday?"

I should tell her how I woke up with it on this morning. How it's clasped so tight I can't even get it off. How it feels like a collar. But the words lodge in my throat, sticking like poison syrup.

If I tell her, she'll think I'm insane. And who wants an insane girl in their space?

I force my expression into something neutral. "Yeah," I lie. "It's... costume jewelry. Probably fake. I found it at a thrift store."

Margaret scoffs. "If that's fake, I'm the Queen of England." She lets the necklace drop against my chest and pats my shoulder. "Seems like someone accidentally sold a family heirloom for cheap."

I laugh, but it's not real. She doesn't notice. She just moves to the fridge, grabbing ingredients, getting back to cooking.

I don't tell her that I can still feel the kiss. Through the blanket. Pressed to the top of my head.

I don't tell her that I think I really might be losing my mind.

Margaret wipes her hands on her apron. "I'll take care of the kitchen prep. But there's a man who just came in; you need to take his order."

I nod, grateful to stay busy. The moment my hands stop moving, my thoughts creep in. I can't let that happen.

I smooth my uniform, grab my notepad, and step into the dining area.

I scan the restaurant, searching for the new customer. He's near the windows, bathed in soft afternoon light, but there's nothing soft about him. His eyes are already on me.

Every step toward him feels like walking toward an execution.

He's handsome, but not in a way that feels safe. His face is all sharp angles and violence. A scar runs from his right ear to his mouth, but it doesn't take away from his looks, it just makes him more striking. More dangerous.

His eyes are as blue as glaciers, and so cold. Despite the menace rolling off him in waves, heat licks up my spine, making me flush. He's huge. His biceps strain against the fabric of his dark sweater, easily twice the size of my head. Everything about him screams danger.

But I have a job to do. I can't just refuse to serve a customer because he looks terrifying.

My hands tremble so badly I worry my notepad will slip, but I hope he doesn't notice. "Hi, welcome. What can I get for you?"

He looks at me like he already knows everything, down to the details of my last cycle.

"You're nervous."

Observant. Great.

"I'm fine. Do you, um, know what you want to order?"

He leans back in his chair, one tattooed arm resting on the table, the other raking through his black hair.

"Busy day?" His voice is smooth and deep, rolling over me like smoke.

I shift on my feet. "Yeah."

"What's your name?"

"Amelia."

"Amelia." He says it like it's familiar.

Weird.

"I really need to take your order." My pitch is too high.

Something dark flickers in his eyes, amusement, interest. A game only he knows the rules to.

"Steak," he finally says. "Rare."

I jot it down quickly. "And to drink?"

"Water." He drawls it out, but his gaze burns through me, leaving me exposed.

"Okay." I mumble, turning fast, eager to flee back to the kitchen.

Margaret works beside me, kneading dough for the next batch of bread.

"That man rattled you," she muses.

I shake my head quickly. "No, just tired."

I make sure the steak is rare; barely cooked in the center. The sight of the raw meat churns my stomach. I've never been a fan.

Margaret notices. "I can do it if you want."

"I got it."

I finish the steak and plate it with a side of roasted potatoes, making sure it's perfect.

Come on, Amelia. You're a big girl. Nothing to be scared of.

Feigning confidence, I walk back to his table and set the plate down. But I don't wait around. I bolt, tending to other customers.

But I still feel him.

Even from across the room, his presence is heavy. Watching.

A while later, he signals for me.

I hesitate.

Margaret nudges me. "Go on, hon. He's just asking for the bill."

Just the bill.

I force my legs to move. My mind goes into fight-or-flight at the sight of him. I don't understand why. But underneath the fear, there's something else...attraction.

Shame crawls up my spine. How can I be terrified of this man and drawn to him at the same time?

I slide the bill onto the table. He takes his time wiping his mouth with a napkin before looking up at me.

"Amelia?"

I hum in response, barely trusting my voice.

His lips curl at the corners. "Wear the dress. It goes well with your necklace."

He doesn't give me time to process before he's out the door.

The world narrows.

How does he know about the dress? My fingers reach for the necklace at my throat, its cold diamonds pressing against my skin. My pulse races.

It's him, isn't it?

Cold sweat clings to my spine.

I pull myself together, pretending everything is fine, and reach for the bill.

When I flip it over, I nearly pass out.

He left a tip.

A huge one.

$1,000.

I feel sick.

Chapter Seven
Damien

Talking to my Amelia for the first time was like setting fire to my own skin. A million fire ants crawling under it, stinging, tearing, burning. My mind was never quiet to begin with, but now it's fucking ruined. She's in my head.

I need to know her. Need to take her apart piece by piece and see what makes her *her*.

But right now, I have business to attend to. Richard Davis has summoned me again.

Richard sits across from me, his daughter draped in a dress that barely qualifies as one. It's something better suited for a strip club than this cigar lounge. Her manicured fingers toy with the rim of her glass like it's the tip of a dick. She's looking at me with her lips pursed, eyes wide, like a fish out of water. If this is her attempt at being seductive, I'd be shocked if she's ever gotten laid in her life.

Richard exhales a cloud of smoke. "Linda asked for you."

I grunt.

She uncrosses her legs, shifting forward. "I need you to kill someone else for me."

"Another job?"

"There's this girl who won't stop running her mouth about me. Always talking behind my back, spreading rumors—"

I tune her out, jaw ticking. A girl? Not a rat. Not a threat. Just some spoiled little princess with a vendetta over gossip.

I turn my gaze to Richard. "I don't do unjustified targets." My voice is cold. "That's a sure way to get lazy. And lazy men get killed."

She pouts, leans in further, giving me a view of what she clearly wants me to see. "Didn't you kill someone for me already? What's another one?"

And there it is. She's overthinking. Twisting it in her head, thinking it meant something personal. It didn't. It never does.

"I'm a hitman. Not a fucking errand boy."

She doesn't like hearing *no*. I can tell no one's ever told her that word in her entire spoiled existence.

Richard laughs, tapping ash from his cigar. "Told you he'd say that." He smirks. "But I've never seen my daughter so bloodthirsty before. Thought it was worth a shot."

Linda crosses her arms. She's pissed. Too bad. I'm not here to coddle overgrown children.

I glance at her once more, bored. I stand, pulling on my jacket. "You want someone dead, make sure they deserve it."

I walk the fuck out of whatever game she thought she was playing. I shake off my irritation, it's irrelevant. The only thing that matters is *her*. My angel. My Amelia. She'll see soon enough that I take care of what's mine. That flimsy bed she slept on? It wasn't fit for a queen. So, I replaced it.

I exposed myself to her tonight, just a little. I gave her a hint, that I'm the monster under her bed, the shadow in her walls. I thought meeting her in the restaurant would make it easier, gentler, but she was still petrified.

She'd better never think of escaping. Not when I've seen her. Not when I've watched the way her foot dangles off the mattress, just barely, teasing me like she wants me to crawl out from underneath and press my mouth to her skin. To taste her fear. To tell her that even monsters fall for softness.

I reach the restaurant, and the back door is locked this time. Good girl, Amelia. A tiny, foolish attempt at keeping me out. I pick the lock in seconds. The scent of warm bread and something sweeter—*her*—wraps around me as I move through the empty kitchen, down the stairs.

The storage room door is heavier than before. She's barricaded it. Again, good girl. Again, not good enough. She doesn't understand that I would walk through fire to get to her.

I shove forward, and the stand she propped against the door crashes to the ground as it swings open violently.

She screams like her soul is being ripped from her body.

My angel is perched on the bed I left her, breath ragged, eyes wide and wild. A knife trembles in her grip, her fingers locked so tight around the handle they've gone white.

That won't do.

I take a slow step inside, drinking in the sight of her fear. Beautiful. Fragile. *Mine.*

"Now, now, Amelia," I murmur. "What are you going to do with that?"

I crawl onto the soft bed like a predator savoring the chase.

"Stay back," she breathes, pressing herself against the headboard.

She could scream, fight, beg; and I would still come to her. I was made for this. For her.

I grab her wrist and guide the blade forward, pressing it to my throat just enough to split the skin. A warm trickle of blood slides down my neck.

"Do it," I whisper with a Cheshire smile. "Cut me open, angel. Spill my blood. Make me yours."

Fire flashes in her eyes, the first flicker of real defiance, and she shoves the blade deeper.

Yes.

For a moment, I think she might actually do it. I almost want her to. But then her body sags, and the fight drains from her bones.

Weak, sweet thing.

I rip the knife from her grip and fling it across the room.

"All I want is to talk," I tell her, my voice dripping with mock patience. I reach for her, brushing a strand of hair behind her ear. She flinches. The reaction slams through me like a bullet to the skull. I want to rip her fear out of her, carve it away with my teeth.

"Talk? You brought me a severed tongue," she screeches. "You sleep under my bed, you maniac."

A grin I can't help splits my lips.

"I do," I say simply.

She recoils as I pull a rope from my waistband and hold it out to her. Her face drains of color.

"If you're so scared," I sigh, "tie me up."

Her throat bobs as she swallows.

"Go on," I press. "Make the knots tight. Unforgiving." I coax her. "If it makes you feel safe, I'll let you."

She thinks it's a trap of some kind; it isn't. She takes the rope with shaking hands. I let her. For her, I'd endure anything. She binds my wrists together tightly so the rope bites into my flesh. The pain is exquisite. She's touching me. That's all that matters.

She steps back to study her work. "That was stupid."

"Was it?" I tilt my head.

"How do you know I won't hurt you?" Her voice gains strength. "Call the police? Run?"

A laugh rips from my throat, low, dark, unhinged.

I lean forward, even with my hands bound, and she stiffens.

"You underestimate me, angel," I say. "Hurt me?" I shake my head. "You don't have it in you."

If looks could kill, my little flower would have successfully killed me.

"Call the police?" I continue. "You don't even have a phone. And every shop on this street is closed. No one to help you. Run? You don't want to run, Amelia." I drink in the scent of her fear, her skin, her everything. "You want answers."

And I'm going to give them to her.

She stares at me like I'm something out of a nightmare. Maybe I am.

"What's your name?"

"Damien. Damien Reed."

"And you," I mumble, "are Amelia Ward. Soon to be Amelia Reed."

"You're insane."

I watch her like a puzzle I've already solved. "You say that like it changes anything."

"Why are you doing this?"

"Doing what? Protecting you?" I ask. "Making sure no one lays a finger on you? Spoiling you the way you deserve?"

I see the conflict in her eyes. There's a part of her that wants to understand.

"Couldn't you just approach me like a normal person?"

A normal person.

"Why would I hide myself from you, Amelia? This is how our life is always going to be."

"If someone hurts you," I continue, my voice dropping lower, "I'll bring you a piece of them. So you'll know I avenged you." I smile. I hope it comes across as comforting, but I know it terrifies her too. "If we argue? If you tell me to sleep somewhere else? I'll crawl under your bed and stay there until you want me back in it. I won't pretend to be something I'm not. I won't lie to you."

"You're insane," she repeats. "Absolutely insane. A maniac."

"Your maniac. I would burn the world for you," I hiss. "I would rip through hell just to bring you to me."

She grips the sheets like they're the only thing holding her together.

She stutters out, "Are... are you the Hellkeeper?"

The words catch me off guard. I frown. "The what?"

"The Hellkeeper."

"No, angel." My fingers graze her thigh, just a whisper of touch. "I'm the man who will bring you heaven."

I make a mental note to research the "Hellkeeper".

She recoils. Good. I like her like this; trying so hard to be strong.

"How many other women have you terrorized?"

"If you mean obsessed over—only you," I say. "And if you think making you drip in diamonds and silk is terrorizing, then you're very, very wrong."

It's the truth. She's the only one who's ever sunk into my bones like this. Other women? They were nothing. Just flesh. A means to an end. A scratch to an itch.

But her? She's fire licking up my spine. A hunger that won't quiet.

Enough of her questions. It's my turn. "Why don't you have any records here?"

"No school history, no university, no doctor visits, no bank accounts." I cock my head. "It's like you're a ghost."

The bewilderment on her face is hilarious.

"I did my research."

"You had no right."

"I answered your questions, didn't I? It's only fair you answer mine."

"I'm not from here." She relents.

I arch a brow. "Then where?"

She hesitates.

"Hell."

I turn the word over in my head. Hell. Hell. It clicks. That little village just outside the city. There are a shit-ton of rumors surrounding it. Lots of people theorize it's a cult. The pieces fall into place. Her naivety. Her shyness. The way she clings to prayers like they're armor.

She ran.

She left them behind; whatever fucked-up things they did to her, whatever lies they poured into her head. The thought of something—anything—terrifying her makes something vicious curl in my chest.

I growl, low and feral. "I am the only one you're allowed to be afraid of, Amelia. Whatever monsters you think are out there, real or not, I will hunt them down. And I will end them."

I mean every word. When she seems to close off again, I put an end to our conversation.

"This was a productive talk, don't you think?"

I flex my wrists, testing the ropes she so carefully tied. Cute. With one sharp pull, the fibers snap like thread.

She screams and bolts for the door. I catch her before she even gets close. My arms wrap around her waist, lifting her clear off the ground. She thrashes, kicks, nails clawing at my skin. I only tighten my hold, dragging her back.

Her body crashes onto the mattress, the sheets tangling around her as I tuck her in like a precious little doll. Her chest heaves, terror painting her delicate features.

"Shhh," I murmur, pressing my lips to her temple. "I told you before, angel; I won't hurt you. Not unless you ask me to."

"Good night." I brush the strands away from her face, watching her pupils blow wide. "You know where to find me."

I rise, moving to my place beneath the bed, where I've been sleeping since I met her. Because I know she isn't ready to have me next to her.

But she will be.

I close my eyes, listening to the frantic beat of her heart, to the sharp little breaths she takes as she forces herself to stay calm. Her foot slips out from the bed. She's trying to escape. I wrap my fingers around her ankle before she even makes it an inch further. She yelps, but I press a lingering kiss to the inside of her foot.

"You will sleep in the bed I spent a fortune on for you tonight," I order. "If I find you anywhere else..." My grip tightens just a little. "You won't like it."

She curls back into the sheets. Smart girl.

Chapter Eight
Amelia

The second I open my eyes, I curse myself. No. No, no, no—how could I fall asleep?! Idiot.

I swore I'd stay awake until morning. Swore I wouldn't close my eyes, not even for a second, so that maniac wouldn't touch me. Or hurt me.

That handsome maniac—*Shut up, Amelia.*

I throw myself off the bed, ignoring the way my knees nearly buckle as I run in the opposite direction. Away from him. My eyes lock on the dark space beneath the frame. No movement. Nothing. I take a step closer, my pulse hammering in my ears. Then another step. Another. Then I drop to my knees and peek under the bed.

It's empty. He's gone.

Good.

Maybe he got bored. Maybe it's another girl's turn for him to torment.

I push to my feet and begin to pace. Should I tell Margaret? What would I even say?

"*Hey, Margaret! Remember how I told you I ran away because my village wanted to sacrifice me? Yeah, well, now I'm saying there's a man sleeping under my bed and cutting off human tongues for me. Crazy, right?"*

Yeah. No.

She'd pat my shoulder, give me a tight smile, and immediately call the cops. And when they showed up and found nothing? They'd assume I was a lunatic. Maybe even send me back *there*.

I turn off my brain and move on autopilot. I take a shower and go through the motions; pretending like it's just another normal day. But as I clean the restaurant, my mind doesn't stop terrorising me. Is this a curse? Did leaving that place doom me to something worse?

...Or—and this is an incredibly stupid thought, one I refuse to acknowledge as anything other than sheer exhaustion—could the Hellkeeper take the shape of a man? Could he be tricking me?

God. I don't know anything anymore. I don't even know if I believe in the village's curse or the Hellkeeper.

All I know is that I'm confused.

And homesick. Even though my village sucked, it was still home. The only one I've ever known. I miss my mother. I miss the peonies that infiltrated that village.

"Morning, sweetheart," Margaret sing-songs with a bright smile.

"Morning."

We fall into our usual easy rhythm. The familiar routine is oddly comforting, pulling me out of my thoughts.

"Breakfast options today?" I ask as I scribble on the menu board.

Margaret hums in thought. "Let's keep it simple. Pancakes with butter, avocado toast, or the special, French toast."

"Sounds good."

There's still this nagging worry in my chest, and before I can stop myself, I blurt, "Can I ask you something weird?"

Margaret pauses mid-step. "Always."

I grip the rag in my hands a little tighter. "Do you think the curse, the one my village believes in, is real?"

Margaret turns fully, her brows lifting. "The Hellkeeper?"

My body locks up, but I nod.

"No, sweetheart. That nonsense isn't real." She laughs like the whole thing is a big, stupid joke.

Even though it's just her opinion, it makes me feel better somehow.

"So," I say, swallowing, "you don't think my life is going to be cursed because I ran away? Or that some… thing is after me?"

Margaret pats my back, warm and reassuring. "I promise that won't happen."

I let out a breath, nodding. "Thanks."

"What brought this up?"

How do I explain that I woke up terrified out of my mind, convinced a monster was hiding under my bed?

I settle for not lying to her, but not telling her the complete truth either.

"I'm stupidly homesick," I admit. "Even though the village was—" I shake my head. "Horrific."

She doesn't judge me. "What do you miss most?"

The answer comes easily.

"My mother," I say quietly. "And the peonies."

Margaret nods like she gets it. "Flowers were always a comfort to me, too."

The conversation shifts after that, flowing back into work, customers, and the hum of the morning rush. But a realization slams into me. I never told her about the Hellkeeper. Just the curse. I open my mouth to ask, but then I shake my head. I must have mentioned it sometime without realizing.

I head toward the girl who just sat down near the window, her order in my hand. She looks about my age, and the first thing I notice is her energy, it's warm and comforting, like that of an angel.

"Here you go," I say, setting the plate in front of her. "French toast. Enjoy."

Her eyes light up. "Oh, wow, this looks delicious. Thank you!"

"Are you new?" she quickly adds when I turn to leave.

"Kind of," I say. "I've been working here for a little while now."

"Well, I'm glad I came in today, then. I'm Ruby, by the way."

"Amelia."

"Nice to meet you, Amelia." She takes a bite of the toast. "Okay, this is so good. I think you just found yourself a regular customer."

"That's good to hear. Margaret—she owns this place—makes everything from scratch. She'll be happy to know it's a hit."

This morning is slower than usual, so we fall into easy conversation. She tells me about her job at a little bakery down the street, how she loves reading but can never find anyone to talk books with. I tell her about working here, how it's nice but busy, and how sweet Margaret is. It's been a while since I've clicked with someone like this.

"You should totally give me your number. We could go out sometime, just talk and get to know each other better."

The moment the words leave her mouth, my stomach twists. *I don't have a phone.*

Insecurity prickles at my skin, and I open my mouth, ready to admit it, until I see the innocent curiosity in her face. I don't want to see pity there.

So I lie.

"Ah, well, my phone's, uh, broken," I say, forcing a sheepish smile. "I'm getting it fixed, though. I'll give you my number then."

Ruby blinks, then laughs. "Oh, gotcha." She winks. "Guess I'll just have to keep coming here for breakfast until you give it to me."

I snort. "Not the worst plan."

She slides a bill under her plate as she stands. "Well, I'll see you soon, Amelia. Don't forget to fix that phone of yours."

"I won't," I say as I walk her to the door.

The second she's gone, another wave of insecurity hits me. I didn't really fit in back in my village, but I want to fit in here. I want somewhere I can belong. That's why I will get a phone. Maybe tomorrow. Damien, my monster, left me a huge tip last time. I can spare a little.

My fingers tighten around my apron.

I called him mine.

I frown.

My monster.

I'm starting to get used to him.

Chapter Nine
Damien

She owns me. Body, mind, and soul. Just like I'm going to own her.

Soon.

Very soon.

I sit in the restaurant before dawn, the only person in the empty space, my fingers drumming against the table as I wait for her to climb the stairs. My blood hums with anticipation. My heart beats for nothing but her. I can already picture the look on her face when she steps inside and sees my gift. She'll see proof that I know her; that I listen to everything she says, even when she doesn't think I'm there. She doesn't see me watching. Doesn't know that every sigh she makes, every little thought she mutters to herself…I know it all.

She'll learn, though, to recognize my presence, to feel when I'm near.

Amelia rushes upstairs with the phone I left on her bedside table clutched to her chest, like it's a sin she still wants it even though she knows it's from me. She takes in the restaurant with a gasp. Her lips part as she drinks in the sight of hundreds of peonies. They're everywhere. In vases, on the counters, tucked into little corners like I wanted her to find them again and again.

"I hope you like my gifts, little flower."

She flinches, spinning toward me, her breath hitching. I drink in her reaction; how her pupils widen when she sees me, how her hands tighten around the gift I left her. She looks so small standing there, like something meant to be kept, held, and cherished.

"Why?" she whispers.

I rise from my seat, savoring the way she tenses as I move toward her. Her body knows before her mind does. Knows that I belong this close. That she was always meant to belong to me. I stop just inches away from her, and reach out to tuck a strand of her hair behind her ear. She shivers.

"You deserve to be spoiled, Amelia," I murmur, caressing the curve of her neck. "You deserve to be worshipped."

She blinks up at me, confused. Naïve. Innocent little thing.

"W-Worshipped?" she stammers.

I hum, my fingers tracing just outside the swell of her breasts. She jerks slightly, but I don't move away. I keep my touch feather-light, teasing. She's too frozen to stop me, too curious about what I might do next.

My breath ghosts against her ear. "Tell me, little flower," I say, trailing my fingers lower, just over her ribs, the dip of her waist. "Do you want to be touched?"

Her nipples pebble beneath her dress.

Fuck.

She gasps, ripping herself away, but I follow, my touch skimming lower.

"Does it confuse you?" I rasp. "The heat between your thighs? The ache?"

My fingers stop just above her hip bone. "I know you're wondering why it's all wet down there."

A strangled sound leaves her throat before she shoves me away. "You're absolutely filthy," she hisses.

I grin. Her innocence is so fucking sweet. I want to drag her down into my filth, cover her in it, and make sure she never finds her way back to the light.

Before I can respond, the door creaks open, and Margaret walks in. I like Margaret. I really do. She took Amelia in, gave her shelter. And for that, she deserves to be spoiled, too.

Her wrinkled hands fly to her chest as she takes in the decorated restaurant. "Oh my goodness!" she gushes. "Amelia! Did you do all this?"

What can she say? *No, my stalker did?* So she nods.

Margaret beams, kissing Amelia's cheek. "It's lovely, sweetheart. Just lovely."

Margaret's eyes widen slightly when she notices me. "Oh?"

"A customer came in early," Amelia explains quickly. "I couldn't turn him away."

Margaret pats her cheek with motherly affection. "Of course, dear. That's good business sense."

Amelia tries to compose herself, but I still see straight through her.

"Well," she sighs, "please take a seat so I can take your order."

This is going to be fun.

"What can I get you?"

"You."

"Damien," she hisses under her breath, eyes flicking to her side like she's scared Margaret is going to materialize there any second.

"Fine," I sigh, dragging my eyes over her body, eating her up. "Eggs. Toast. Black coffee. And you."

She exhales sharply, looking anywhere but at me. "Just the first three," she mutters, scribbling it down.

She shifts from foot to foot, those pretty thighs pressing together just so.

"You keep moving like that, flower," I say lazily, "and I'm going to start thinking about why."

"What?"

"You want something," I tell her. "I can see it. Feel it. I bet if I touched you right now, if I spread those little thighs of yours, I'd find you soaking for me."

"Stop it," she orders, but there's no conviction behind it.

"You want me to stop?" I tilt my head. "Or do you want me to tell you more? Tell you exactly what your body is craving?"

She's crumbling.

And she doesn't even know it yet.

She flees to the kitchen.

You won't run for long, my sweet little flower.

The morning rush starts, but my girl isn't quite the same.

She shuffles on her feet, tugs at her apron, presses her thighs together as she scribbles down orders. Her skin is flushed, her breath just a little too shallow.

She knows I'm still watching her.

She likes it.

The girl from yesterday walks in. The one Amelia clicked with.

I lean back in my seat, watching as they exchange smiles and soft laughter.

My beautiful girl is making friends. Good.

I watch as she gives her number to this new friend. Something dark and possessive coils in my gut, but I force myself to breathe.

She's allowed to have friends.

I want her to have friends.

Because at the end of the day, when she's writhing under me, begging for my touch, I'll be the only one who knows her the way she needs to be known.

She can make as many friends as she wants. She'll still belong to me.

When she sets my order in front of me, I don't touch the food.

My appetite is singular.

I lift the cup of coffee, taking a slow sip, my eyes never leaving hers. The bitterness rolls over my tongue.

"Good," I praise, licking a stray drop from my lip. "But I bet you'd taste better."

She furrows her brows, her confusion almost adorable.

My poor, sheltered girl. She doesn't even understand what I mean.

"What?"

"Don't worry, little flower. You'll learn soon enough."

"Stop talking like that."

"Like what? Like I want to spread you open on this table and bury my tongue so deep inside you, you'll forget your own name?"

The horror in her eyes is delicious.

"No way." She stumbles back a step.

I laugh, setting the cup down. She turns to flee again, but I'm faster, pressing a firm hand against her stomach, fingers resting just above the band of her apron.

"You grew up religious, didn't you?" I coax. "A village full of good little girls and boys. Let me guess…

they taught you that a man only takes his wife to bed to put a baby in her? That it happens in the dark, under the covers, over in seconds?" I chuckle darkly, my hand sliding just a little lower. Not touching where she's aching, but close. "That won't be us, Amelia."

Her fingers twitch at her sides.

She wants to run.

She wants to stay.

"When I take you," I whisper, "you'll be spread out for me, bare in the light. My tongue will know every inch of you before my cock even touches you. I'll make you beg for things you don't even understand yet."

"Enough," she chokes out.

"Do you feel that, little flower?" I press just a bit firmer. "That pulse between your thighs? It's me. You want my touch. And when I do touch you—" I inhale deeply, letting her scent fill my lungs. "—you'll wonder how you ever lived without it."

Chapter Ten
Amelia

I can't believe this man. This monster.

He's awakened something inside me; something I never even realized existed. And now... now I want something twenty-four/seven, and I don't even know what it is.

I just know that it aches. That it hurts. That I'm so frustrated I could scream.

It's been two days since he littered this place with peonies and gave me the phone I wanted, but he hasn't visited the restaurant since. He still sleeps in the same room as me. I feel him there, lingering in the walls, in my sheets, in the spaces I leave behind. But he hasn't revealed himself. No more conversation. No more heated words that leave me burning from the inside out.

Something must be wrong with me.

Because I miss him.

And I want him to fix whatever mess he caused between my thighs.

I press my lips together, my fingers toying with the diamond pendant around my neck. Is what he said true? That the village, the people, the way we were raised, it's all a lie? The elders always held lectures, hammering into our heads that pleasure was indulgence, indulgence was weakness, and weakness led straight into the devil's hands. Even in marriage, there were rules, modesty, restraint, duty above desire.

And yet, he speaks of it like it's something else entirely. Something I was meant to crave.

I put on my best smile as I turn to greet the customer who just walked in, only for it to falter slightly. She doesn't look like she belongs here. Tall, elegant, draped in diamonds, she's probably the most gorgeous woman I've ever seen.

My fingers brush over my necklace again. His gift. How am I supposed to make sense of my feelings when the man who stalks me, taunts me, and invades every part of my life is also the one who spoils me?

I shake the thought away. "Welcome. Would you like a table?"

She completely ignores me, giving the place a once-over. Something close to disgust twists her beautiful features into ugliness before she makes her way to an empty table like she's gracing us with her presence.

I ignore her rudeness. "What can I get you?"

She looks at me like I've personally offended her, which isn't possible as I've literally just met the woman. "Just a coffee. Black. No sugar."

No sugar? Yeah, that tracks. She probably diets hard to maintain her figure. If she wanted just coffee, the café next door would've been the more logical choice, but of course, I keep that to myself.

I nod, jotting it down. Before I can leave, she lifts a manicured hand.

"You work here full-time?"

I glance down at my stained apron, then back at her. "That's right."

"That's... nice."

The pause is just long enough to make it clear it isn't.

"I expected you to be more," she says nonchalantly, flipping her perfect blonde hair back.

What does that even mean? I don't even know her. "I'm sorry?"

She waves a delicate hand. "Oh, nothing. Forget it."

She gives me a smile that's all teeth. "I admire people like you. So content with what they have. Simple things. Simple lives."

Ouch. Clearly, that was a dig.

"I suppose it's a gift. Some people spend their whole lives wanting things they can't have."

It just felt like the right thing to say at the moment, because even though this woman looks perfect, there's something about her that drips with desperation. She's desperate. For what? I don't know. I have no idea why she's projecting that desperation onto me, but it doesn't make me insecure, it just makes me sad for her.

I leave her stewing and return with her coffee. She doesn't touch it right away, just sits there, stirring slowly, watching me.

I don't let it get to me.

Eventually, she lifts the cup and takes a sip. She sets it down, dabbing at her red-tinted lips with a napkin. "It's bitter."

I shrug. "It's what you ordered."

Her eyes narrow. But she doesn't say anything else. Instead, she grabs her purse, throws a couple of bills on the table, and leaves.

Weird woman.

The rest of the day passes in a blur of customers and the occasional strange interaction, though nothing quite as bizarre as that blonde woman. By the time the restaurant closes, my feet ache and my brain is mush.

I grab a rag, wipe down the last table, and head to the back. I kick off my shoes, plop down on the mattress, and let out a deep sigh. The mattress Damien got me feels like sleeping on a cloud.

Like an idiot with zero survival instincts, I pop my head under the bed, checking if he's there. He's not.

What if he's the devil?

I mean… it sounds stupid. I know it sounds stupid. But the elders always warned us that temptation came dressed in wicked beauty, and he's definitely that.

And just to be safe…

I grab the bundle of sage I keep in the drawer, light the end, and hold it out in front of me as I walk around the room, waving it through the air like some kind of exorcist.

"Alright, you demon. If you're in here, get out."

I waft the smoke extra hard into the corners.

My prayers are getting rusty, the longer I'm away from the village, the more hollow they feel on my tongue.

Nothing happens. Which is exactly what I expected but also vaguely disappointing.

I turn, pointing the smoldering sage at the door. "If there is an evil entity here, leave through this door and never return."

And that's when it swings open. I yelp, nearly launching the sage straight at him.

He catches my wrist before I can commit arson. "The hell are you doing?"

I stare up at Damien, heartbeat pounding. He's close. Too close. His fingers are warm where they curl around my skin, and his eyes flick between me and the still-smoking bundle in my hand.

I swallow. "...Cleansing the room?"

His lips twitch. "You think I'm some kind of ghost?"

No, but—

Maybe.

I wrench my arm back and step away. "Demon, actually. Possibly the Hellkeeper himself."

A beat of silence. Then, he laughs.

I glare. "This is serious."

He's still grinning. "And you thought sage would keep me away?"

"Maybe? Besides, if you were here from the start, why not pop out sooner?"

"Maybe I just like watching you act like a little lunatic."

I bristle, puffing up. "I am not a lunatic. I was just raised with certain values and beliefs."

"Speaking of values and beliefs, tell me, little flower. Have you been thinking about what I said?"

My breath catches. Because the answer is yes. Constantly. And judging by the way his lips curl, he already knows it.

I busy myself stuffing the sage back into the drawer. "No."

"It eats at you, doesn't it?"

"I don't know what you're talking about."

"You do."

He steps behind me, not quite touching, but there. "You're curious."

I hate how easily he sees through me. This has got to be the dumbest moment of my life. I should be screaming. I should be running. I should be doing something other than sitting on my bed talking to the man who stalked me like we're old friends catching up.

But instead, I hear myself turn the conversation to something I'm more comfortable with. Because again, like the idiot I am, I want to talk to him. "What do people in the city do for fun?"

Damien stares at me like I just asked him to recite the scriptures.

I sigh. "What? I'm serious. Back home, there wasn't much to do except read, sew, and pray. If you didn't do those, you were 'straying from the light.'"

"You strayed, didn't you?"

"Clearly."

"To answer your question… People drink. They go to clubs. They fight. They waste time."

I frown. "That sounds awful."

"Depends on the person."

"What do you do?"

"I watch you."

My stomach twists, but I force myself to roll my eyes. "That's not a real answer."

"It is to me."

I groan. "Okay, let me try again. If you had to do something normal, something that didn't involve tracking my every move, what would it be?"

"I go shooting sometimes."

"Like… with a gun?"

"Yes, little flower. With a gun."

"Of course Mr. Mysterious Stalker Man can't have a normal hobby."

"Mr. Mysterious Stalker *Husband*."

Huh?

"What?"

He sits on the bed next to me. "Not only a stalker, Amelia. Your future husband, too."

I chew on my lip, choosing to ignore his nonsense. "We weren't allowed to have those back home. They said weapons only belong in the hands of demons."

Damien chuckles, dark and low. "Then you'd hate my collection."

I stare at him. He stares back, completely unfazed. This is my life now.

I rub my temples. "God, I need therapy." I'd heard that word used by many teenage girls in the restaurant, and when Margaret explained it to me, I decided that yes—teenage girls, me too.

"I can be your therapy."

I point a finger at him. "Stop trying to be flirty."

He shrugs like he's physically incapable of not flirting with me.

"Alright, your turn. Ask me something," I say. I need to admit that I don't want the conversation to end with him. I wish we could have something normal, but it's clear that neither he nor I are that. Why not pretend for now?

He thinks for a moment. "What's the worst thing you've ever done?"

I should lie and say something harmless, like sneaking extra food from the communal pantry. But instead, I find myself telling the truth. "I ran away."

"Do you regret it?" he asks.

"I don't know."

For a long moment, he says nothing. Then, softly—"I've run away too."

"From what?" I blurt out, wanting someone to relate to me desperately.

He doesn't answer. Instead, he watches me, dark eyes burning into mine. And I realize that this is the longest we've talked without me trying to escape.

Chapter Eleven
Damien

My little flower is a narcotic. My little flower is a drug. My little flower is my high, everything I could ever need or want.

I breathe, sleep, and eat this girl. She's carved into my bones, woven into my blood. If someone cut me open, her name would pour out. She's the only person in this godforsaken world I've ever opened up to; and the only one I ever will.

She doesn't know it yet, but I'll tell her everything. Just like she'll tell me all of her secrets. There will be nothing between us. We are one.

I'm giving her time to understand this. To let the truth seep into her skin, to let it settle into her soul. But it's getting harder.

Harder to pretend I don't notice the way she bites her lip when she's thinking.

Harder to act like I don't see the heat creeping up her neck when I lean in too close.

Harder not to pin her down and show her exactly how her man can worship her; how he can make her feel like the goddess she is.

I want to kneel at her feet, lap at her essence, and thank her for letting my filthy hands touch her pure skin. I want to ruin her so completely that when she closes her eyes, the only thing she sees is me.

I want her moaning my name in prayer, whispering it like it's the only salvation she has left.

But for now, I wait.

The rifle is steady in my hands, pressed firm against my shoulder as I watch my target. I haven't been able to accompany my girl to work these past few days as I've been catching up on all the hits I'd ignored in favor of sleeping under her bed.

My eyes never stray from Edward Moore. One of the biggest drug dealers in the underground. You wanted a hit of something rare? He had it.

Had being the key word.

Because Edward Moore decided to repent. Decided to go clean. Decided he could screw over the very people who made him, missing shipments to gangs who had already paid.

Now, they all want him dead.

And who better for the job than me?

I exhale, lining up the shot. He's sitting in his car, oblivious that these are his final seconds. My finger tightens on the trigger, and I fire. The bullet finds its mark, right between his eyes. He crumples instantly, slumping forward onto the wheel, a fine mist of red splattering the windshield.

The job is done.

And now, I have something far more important to return to.

My little flower is waiting.

The moment I pull onto the main road, my phone vibrates. Unknown number. Not uncommon as most of my clients use burners, keeping their names and sins hidden. I answer without a second thought.

"Damien?" a woman sing-songs.

My brows furrow as I try to place her. Lina? Luna? Something with an L.

She answers the unspoken question. "It's Linda."

Ah.

The blonde with the diamonds and the entitled attitude. The one who, despite being old enough to know better, still believes the world bends to her will.

I don't respond. I wait.

"I was thinking about you," she purrs. "We had such a connection, don't you think?"

This woman is either delusional or stupid.

"What. Do. You. Want." My voice is a growl, stripped of patience.

She laughs like I'm teasing her. "Oh, Damien, don't be so cold."

My irritation edges toward something dangerous. "I don't do small talk. What the fuck do you want?"

There's a pause. Then she tries again, her voice syrupy and false. "I just thought... maybe we could see each other outside of business."

Rage floods me. It's ice-cold and blinding.

"That's never going to happen." My words slice through her delusion.

She shrieks in outrage, the sound grating in my ear.

Before I can end the call, she blurts, "Wait! I have another hit I need you to do."

Does she think I'll humor her just because her daddy pays me for a couple of hits?

My teeth grind together. "Let your father communicate it to me."

"But—"

"Any more of this nonsense and tell Richard I won't pick up another job for him. Ever."

She exhales sharply. "Fine."

I hang up before she can say another word. If she thinks she can dangle work over my head to get what she wants, she's dead wrong. I don't need their money. I've got seven figures stacked away. Investments that multiply by the second. If I wanted to, I could put down the rifle today and never touch it again.

No one holds anything over me anymore.

And I will never, *ever*, belong to anyone but my little flower.

I arrive and sneak in like usual.

My little flower is lying in that pathetic excuse of a room, fast asleep. The world isn't ready for what I'll become if I have to keep watching her work her fingers to the bone and sleep in a fucking storage room.

She needs to let me in.

This is all I have...*her*. The obsession. The addiction. The hunger that gnaws at my insides. It's all-consuming. It threatens to break me apart.

But not yet.

 Not until I have her.

I open one of the drawers next to her bed, suppressing the violent emotions I feel at how little she owns. That won't do. My girl deserves the world. White cotton panties catch my eye. I fist them in my hand, bringing them to my face and sniffing like a rabid dog. But it smells like nothing but detergent.

Disappointing.

I want to *smell* her. *Taste* her. I want what's between her lush little thighs.

She stirs, slowly waking up. Those wide, innocent eyes blink open. Confusion clouds her face for a moment before realization hits. She shoots upright, the thin sheet sliding off her body.

"What are you doing?" Her voice is groggy.

I lift the scrap of cotton between my fingers. "These were in your drawer. So clean. So pure. That won't last long, little flower."

And it won't. I'm going to fuck her so thoroughly, she'll never find a pair of clean panties again. Everything she presses between her legs will be soaked with my seed.

She turns bright red, like a rose. "Give those back," she hisses; but I don't miss the flicker of curiosity in her eyes.

"Come and take them."

She shakes her head. Like she *knows* what'll happen if she gets closer.

I crouch down in front of her. "You're afraid of me," I murmur, letting my knuckles graze her thighs. "But not enough to run."

"I—"

"Hush." I place a finger on her soft lips. "I want to teach you something."

"Teach me what?"

I grin. Dark. Satisfied.

"Everything."

She trembles with a mix of fear and something else. Something hotter.

"What do you mean?"

"You're so innocent," I grunt. "You don't even realize the power you have over me, do you? You make me lose control."

"How do I do that? I'm not trying to," she mutters, pouting, confused.

She doesn't even have to try. She could wiggle a finger at me, and I'd drop to my knees.

The fabric of her nightgown clings to her skin, her nipples hard and visible through the thin material; begging to be sucked.

I guide her hands to my waist. Her fingers hover at my waistband, hesitant, but she doesn't pull away. I guide her hand lower until she feels the hardness of my cock through my jeans.

"This is what you do to me," I whisper, barely holding myself back. She's been sheltered. She doesn't know anything about men. And she won't, no one but me.

Her fingers twitch, grazing against me. "Do you understand now?" I ask, pressing her hand a little firmer. "*You're* the reason I'm like this."

"Why is it... why does it happen when I'm near you?" It's like she's trying to understand something too big, too overwhelming.

I tilt her chin up to look at me. "Because you're everything I want, little flower. You're everything I need."

Reluctantly, I move her hand to my chest. "Feel that?" I hum. "Feel how fast my heart is beating? That's because of you. You make me feel alive."

After a long, heated silence, her voice is barely a whisper.

"And when you... feel like this... what happens?"

"I suffer," I say. "I crave relief. But more than that, I crave *you*."

I study the flush blooming up her neck, the subtle way her thighs shift.

"And how do you…?" She's unsure how to phrase it. But I know exactly what she's asking.

"Watch me," I command.

I give her a moment to absorb what's happening. Then I begin. I reach down, unzipping my jeans, and free my cock. Shock floods her face. I'd bet my entire fortune she's never seen one before.

That fact pleases me *immensely*.

"Let me explain," I say. "This… part of me, my cock, it reacts. You can see it. The way it pulses. The way it aches."

I stroke myself slowly, loving how she can't decide whether to look at my face or my cock.

"Yeah, little flower. Enjoy it. Look at it. It's the only cock you'll ever know."

I move faster now, working myself hard. The air is thick with tension. Her confusion. Her curiosity. Her arousal. It's intoxicating.

I'm close. So fucking close. "Watch me," I grunt. "Watch how your man spills, how he breaks for you."

The wave crashes. White floods my vision. I come, hot and thick. Her name is a mantra on my lips.

Amelia. My *Amelia*. My little flower.

I aim for the underwear I took from her drawer. The fabric now holds *all of me*. All of my come.

I hold it out to her, the evidence of my release still fresh on the material.

"Wear it," I order. "Let your pussy get accustomed to the seed it will take for the rest of its lifetime."

She bites her lip, fidgeting with her fingers. I know her, she can't decide whether to cling to her innocence, to her sanity, or to the way I make her pussy drip.

She fights with herself a little longer before making her decision. Slowly, she slides the underwear she's wearing off, letting it drop to the floor. She does it properly; in a way that doesn't let me see what's mine between her legs.

I don't miss the irony.

With a trembling hand, she picks up the pair I've offered her.

She slides it on, bathing her little cunt in her stalker's release. She shudders as she adjusts herself, not yet accustomed to the feel of her monster.

The hunger in me intensifies. Before she can stop me, I lunge for the pair she took off; the ones that were pressed against her cunt.

I grip them, pulling them to my face, and groan, the sound primal and desperate. I inhale her scent like an animal, my lips brushing against the fabric. I lick and suck at it, tasting her essence.

I want to taste it straight from the source, but I need her more desperate for me before I do that. I need her so horny she won't resist.

Fuck, I'm an animal for this woman, and I don't care who sees or knows.

Chapter Twelve
Amelia

Incineration. Fire. Hell. That's all that's flowing through my veins.

He rocked my world yesterday, did things I never thought were appropriate, but I couldn't stop him for the life of me. I wanted it. I wanted to watch my stalker unravel for me. And after all that, he just slept on the floor next to my bed, not giving me what I wanted, leaving me with something I don't know how to deal with. Hot and bothered between the legs. I couldn't sleep all night, hot flashes attacking me every time I shifted and felt his mess in my underwear.

It's Saturday, and Margaret has given me the day off. I exchanged numbers with Ruby last week; the customer I clicked with. I'm still not used to the phone and sometimes forget I even own it, but thankfully I saw her text to hang out.

We meet at the bookstore down the street. Ruby is already waiting for me near the fiction section, and my senses are assaulted by the scent of old paper and vanilla that seems to stick to this place.

"Hello!" she sing-songs like the sunshine she is.

I set my heavy bag down on a nearby table. "I've been looking forward to this all day, Ruby," I say.

She nudges me playfully. "Good. Because I intend to make sure you leave here with at least five books."

I glance at the overflowing stack in her arms. "I take it you read a lot?"

"Please, books are my first love." She rolls her eyes dramatically. "You ever get lost in one? Like, really lost?"

"Not really. I mean, I've read, but..." I trail off.

"Don't tell me you've never read a romance book."

I shift awkwardly. "I haven't."

She acts like I've personally insulted her, which is awful because I really enjoy her company and want her to enjoy mine too. "You're missing out on a lot."

"Aren't all genres basically the same? I mean, books are books."

"No. Absolutely not. There's angst, heartbreak, spice—" She pauses, narrowing her eyes at me. "Wait. You do know about the spice, right?"

"Spice? Of course, Ruby, I literally work at a restaurant." I'm confused as to what spice has to do with anything with books.

She doubles over with laughter. "Oh my God. Not that type of spice!"

"What type then? I mean, there are a lot—cumin, ginger, paprika..." I start listing them off using my fingers.

"Oh, this is going to be so much fun." Ruby manages out between fits of laughter.

She scans the titles before plucking a few books from the shelves and handing them to me.

"These," she declares, "will change your life."

I glance down at the covers. My face burns instantly.

"Ruby," I whisper-shout. "These men are half-naked."

"And? Trust me, Amelia, it's not just about the covers. What's inside is even better."

Curiosity gets the better of me, so I follow Ruby to the register, wondering what exactly I've just gotten myself into.

***

Walking back to the restaurant with those books feels like a walk of shame. I'm a mess of nerves by the time I reach my room. I drop onto my bed, clutching the book in my hands. The second I flip open the first page, I'm sucked in. My eyes widen at every detail.

People do those things?

When I think about it objectively, it's crude. Gross, even. But when I think of doing these things with Damien… I melt. Something must be wrong with me.

And that's exactly when the door suddenly bursts open. I jolt upright, the book nearly flying from my hands.

"You are getting way too comfortable with breaking and entering," I sigh. Is it even breaking and entering at this point if I expect him to come and am excited for it?

He shoves his hands in his pockets like this is the most casual thing in the world. "Stop pretending you don't like it."

I roll my eyes. "The stalking?"

"What about it?"

I open my mouth to retort, but his gaze flicks downward to the book I'm reading. A book with a shirtless man on the cover, his muscles glistening.

Damien goes completely still. "What the fuck is that?"

"What does it look like, Damien? It's a novel."

His nostrils flare. "A novel," he repeats. "That's what they're calling this filth now?"

"It's not filth."

(It is, but a little white lie never hurt anyone.)

"Then tell me, little flower, what exactly are you learning from this?"

I refuse to answer.

In two strides, he's on me, yanking the book from my hands and flipping through the pages.

"Sit down."

"Damien—"

"Sit," he commands, his voice as hard as stone.

Something in me obeys before my mind can catch up. God, my body responds to this man before my mind does.

"Let's see what's got you so red in the face."

"*His mouth worshiped every inch of her, savoring the taste of her—*"

"Oh my God, stop!" I practically throw myself forward to snatch the book from his grasp. He catches me midair like some hulk and pulls me against him.

He tosses the book onto the bed. "You'd rather learn from some pathetic fiction than from me?"

I gape at him. This man is mentally unwell. So am I, because I'm attracted to him.

"It's just a book."

"A book that made you blush. A book that possibly made your pussy drip."

" Why are you so mad?"

His thumb brushes my lower lip. "Because no one gets to teach you about this but me. After I've taught you everything, every filthy, beautiful thing there is to know, you can read however much of it you want. Just let me be the one who shows you first."

What does he plan on doing? I find out a second later.

"Little flower, I'm going to eat your pussy till you pass out."

"That's so gross," I blurt out without thinking. My brain-to-mouth filter evaporates around this man.

"Gross?" His eyes burn with something dangerous.

"Yes," I answer truthfully, seeing no point in lying.

He lunges at me, yanking my dress up to expose me. A choked sound escapes me.

"Damien, stop," I rasp, pressing my thighs together.

"I'm going to teach you how to love my tongue on your pussy, little flower. I'm going to show you how good it feels."

He rips my underwear off, forcing my legs apart with ease, spreading me open.

"Fucking beautiful," he growls. "Don't you dare hide from me."

Without warning, he licks.

The first lick—oh God. My hips buck involuntarily, chasing his mouth. My body feels like it's on fire.

"You... you can't. It's dirty." My voice cracks. "What if you get sick?"

"It's fucking pure, little flower. You're pure."

His tongue flicks against me again, deeper this time. My entire body reacts against my will.

"You taste so fucking good," he growls. He flicks the tip of his tongue against my ball of nerves, making my back arch. His mouth works over me relentlessly, his hands holding me still as I try to squirm away.

How can I hate this? How can I want this when I told myself I wouldn't?

His mouth fully engulfs me, and the air is knocked out of my lungs as he licks me from bottom to top. My resistance slips away. My hands grasp at his hair, pulling him closer. The pressure between my legs is unbearable.

He pulls back just enough to look up at me, his mouth glistening with evidence of how much I've already given him.

"I told you, little flower. Your body wants this. You need this."

"Please," I whisper. "Please don't stop. I can't…"

I can't finish the sentence, can't say what I want. Because I know how much I'm going to lose myself to him if he keeps going.

My body jerks uncontrollably as something deep inside me unravels. My head spins. It feels so good.

"Shhh, you're fine," he says. "You've been needing this."

When my release fades, I'm left dizzy and disoriented. His touch is much softer now, nothing like before. It's like he wants to soothe me. He cradles me like I'm fragile, rocking me back and forth. "It's okay. You're supposed to like it."

"You're perfect," he murmurs again. "Such a good girl for me. You'll get used to this. You're meant to want this, to want me. And you'll love every second of it."

Chapter Thirteen
Damien

My little flower. My Amelia. My little innocent girl I'm going to corrupt.

It's a crime that she thinks she doesn't taste good. It makes my blood boil that they conditioned her to think she's dirty, unwanted. The very idea is repulsive. She tastes like honey, like flowers, and my mouth waters right now just thinking about it. I should be between her thighs again. Face down, preferably.

I sit on her bed, waiting. The restaurant closed late tonight. I don't like it. She works too much when I could lay the world at her feet and watch her exist in luxury. The thought of her straining herself, being exhausted when she should be resting—when she should be letting *me* take care of her—puts a tight, iron grip on my chest.

Soon.

I hear her soft footsteps in the hall before she finally steps inside. She stops short when she sees me. She no longer startles. *Good girl.* She's getting used to me. Making friends with the monster under her bed.

She rolls her eyes, tossing her apron onto the chair. "Don't you get sick of me?"

Never. Not even a little. Not even for a second. "No."

She clicks her tongue, walking past me to grab a water bottle. She doesn't ask me to leave anymore. She doesn't pretend to be surprised when I show up, doesn't threaten to call the cops, and doesn't act like she doesn't like it.

That's what progress looks like.

Her eyes flicker past me. A box sits on her bed, a bright red dress draped across the top. Beside it, a pair of sleek heels. Excitement flashes across her face for just a second before she forces it down.

My girl loves gifts. And I love gifting her.

She points her water bottle at me. "What's that?"

"If you think I forgot about you refusing to wear the dress I got you, you're mistaken."

"You hold grudges."

I lean back on my hands. "Maybe you didn't like the first one. So I got you another."

"You didn't have to."

"I wanted to."

She flops onto the bed beside the box. I reach for the dress first, dragging my fingers along the material.

"Wear it for me."

She scoffs. "For you?"

"For me." I smile. "And for yourself."

"What's the occasion?"

I watch her, knowing exactly how this next part will go.

"I'm taking you on a date."

"A what?"

"A date, Amelia."

She laughs like this is just a joke. "What, like a normal date?"

"What's funny?"

She sits up fully, crossing her legs. "You. You, Damien."

I grin. "Why?"

She gestures vaguely at me. "Because you're *you*. You're—" She makes a vague, circular motion with her hands. "You show up in my room in the middle of the night, you follow me everywhere, you leave me gifts like some kind of deranged secret admirer. And don't think I forgot about the tongue. Now, all of a sudden, you want to take me on a date? Like whatever's between us is normal?"

"Amelia," I warn.

"Damien." She mimics my tone.

"Put on the dress."

She shakes her head, but she's already holding the dress up against her body, studying herself in the mirror.

My little flower doesn't even realize she's blooming for me. She wants this. She just doesn't know how to let herself have it. Guilt flickers across her face before she pushes it down, pretending she isn't considering it. Pretending she doesn't want to wear my gift, slip into something I chose for her, let me wrap my obsession around her body like silk.

She's trying so hard to fight it.

"Whether you want it or not, you will be going. So let it be your own choice."

Her lips part, eyes snapping to mine. I see it there—hesitation, defiance, longing. She needs the illusion of control, of resistance, so she can pretend this isn't her willingly walking into my world. Willingly facing the real world with her arm wrapped around her monster.

But it is. I know her better than she knows herself.

She rolls her eyes. "Ugh, *fine*. Leave so I can get dressed."

I don't move.

She narrows her eyes. "*Come on!*"

"No."

"Yes," she hisses back.

I arch a brow. "I've seen... *all* of you," I murmur, letting my gaze drag down her body, lingering where I know she's burning. "This is nothing compared to that."

Fire rushes up her throat, blooming across her cheeks. Her hands fist at her sides.

"You're adorable when you're shy, little flower."

"Get out."

"I will undress you myself, Amelia," I threaten.

She sucks in a breath, recoiling from me like she hates the idea. I wait, giving her the illusion of choice.

"Turn around," she mutters with a pout, finally making her decision.

Compromise doesn't sound too bad, so I oblige. I give her my back, even though every cell in my body resists.

She hesitates before the rustling of fabric fills the room. I imagine her delicate fingers tracing over her smooth, unblemished skin as she undresses. I imagine the way her clothes pool at her feet, leaving her in nothing but lace. My breathing turns shallow.

I hear her struggle with the zipper of the dress, huffing in frustration.

"Let me," I say, turning back to face her.

She stills.

My hands find her waist, my fingers caressing her back before I dip my head to it.

She jolts, breath hitching. I press my mouth to her spine. Kissing. Licking. Dragging my teeth across every inch of her skin. My marks bloom against her. Her knees buckle, but my arm wraps around her stomach, holding her up, not letting her fall. She will never fall while with me.

"You don't get to hide from me, Amelia," I mumble around a mouthful of her skin. "Not your body. Not your pleasure. Not the way you tremble when I touch you."

"Oh Damien," she wails.

"Mine," I growl. I press one last open-mouthed kiss to the base of her neck before finally pulling the zipper up.

She sways on her feet, the pleasure I wrung from her still thick in her veins. It clouds her mind. I kneel to slip her sneakers off, massaging her small feet. She nearly moans, but bites her tongue to stop it. I peel her socks off next, my lips brushing against both of her ankles before I slide the heels onto her feet.

She shivers, and I smile.

I rise, watching her take her first cautious step. She wobbles. My hands are on her instantly, steadying her.

"Perhaps heels weren't the wisest choice," I say.

"You bought them."

"Yes." My fingers flex on her waist. "Because I enjoy pushing you out of your comfort zone."

She gasps. "You're—"

I scoop her up before she can finish whatever insult she was about to hurl my way.

Her arms fly around my neck. I relish the way she clings to me.

"Put me down," she demands, though it lacks any real heat.

"No."

"This is ridiculous."

"What's ridiculous," I counter, "is that you insist on resisting when we both know you want to be in my arms."

"I hate you."

"Mmm." I smirk. "Then why are you smiling?"

"I am not."

"You are."

She can deny it all she wants, but I see the truth in every little unconscious action. She is mine.

I set her down beside my Porsche, her balance still unsteady, and open the door. I buckle her seatbelt for her, my face so close to hers I could kiss her. I lean in...

She turns her head.

"Still shy," I remind myself, not letting it get to me.

I round the car, sliding into the driver's seat. As we pull onto the road, I let my palm settle on her thigh. She tenses. Her shoulders reach for her ears, like she can make herself smaller, like she can disappear.

"You wound me, little flower," I sigh. "My touch is meant to make you flourish, not wither away."

"Soon," I continue, "you'll stop shying away. You'll open your legs for me, flutter your lashes, and tell me exactly what you want."

***

I guide her inside the restaurant, leading her toward the VIP section I reserved.

"Why are we sitting here?"

"Privacy," I say simply, pulling out her chair. "I don't like sharing."

She rolls her eyes but sits, eyeing me as I take my place across from her.

I rest my chin on my palm, studying her.

"Stop looking at me like that," she mutters.

"Like what?"

"Like…" She gestures vaguely. "That."

"I enjoy looking at you."

"You enjoy making me uncomfortable."

"Yes," I admit easily. "But mostly, I enjoy you."

Her mouth falls open, caught off guard by my honesty.

"I don't just crave your body, little flower," I confess. "I crave your voice. Your thoughts. Your ideas. Your presence."

"Is it too late for you to set your eyes on someone else?"

"Too late." My right eye twitches. "I'm thoroughly ruined for anyone else. The thought of anyone else is enough to piss me off, so don't bring it up again, little flower."

Her throat bobs as she swallows.

She's starting to realize, isn't she?

That I'm not just obsessed with her.

I'm consumed.

I don't even let her glance at the menu, I don't want her burdened by choices, by something as insignificant as deciding between plates. So I order everything.

The waiter stares at me like I have two heads, but I barely register him. My eyes are locked on her. She's fidgeting with her napkin. I pry it from her hands, threading my fingers through hers.

She doesn't pull away. That's enough to make my pulse hammer against my ribs, to make something sick and satisfied coil deep in my gut.

I have her.

Not fully. Not yet.

But soon.

When the food arrives, it floods the table, plate after plate set down between us. She shakes her head at the obscene amount of food.

"You're insane," she mutters.

"I'm what you made me."

She's unable to hide the way her lips twitch.

I pick up a fork and stab into a piece of seared steak. "Open your mouth."

"I can feed myself."

"Oh, but you won't."

Her lips part in protest, but I use that moment to slide the bite between them. She chews with her brows furrowed, like she's trying to convince herself she doesn't like me pampering her.

This.

This is how I want her.

Mine to feed. Mine to care for. Mine in every possible way.

We fall into easy banter: her trying to resist, me pushing until she gives in. I make her taste everything, watching her reactions like they hold the secrets of the universe.

But her tone shifts in an instant.

"Remember last time," she says, twirling the stem of her glass between her fingers, "you told me you ran away."

A flush creeps up her neck. "From what?"

No secrets between us.

I force the words up my throat, past the barriers I've spent years constructing, past the wounds I've stitched closed with iron will and cruelty.

"I was born to addicts," I say. But I'm detached, like I'm reciting someone else's history. "They left me on the doorstep of some orphanage. I never knew them. Never wanted to."

She's silent, hanging onto every word.

"When I was fourteen, a man adopted me."

She exhales, relieved, like this part of the story might be better.

It isn't.

"He trained me," I continue. "Not to be a son. Not to be a boy. To be something else entirely. Something ruthless."

I feel her move to pull her hands away.

No.

Panic grips me, fast and brutal.

I lash out before she can slip from my grasp, my hands clamping around hers.

"If you run after what I tell you, I don't know what I'll do with myself," I hiss. My voice is sharp, almost venomous, but there's a plea underneath. A desperation. "Don't be scared of me, little flower. Please. Don't be scared of me."

She nods, her hand squeezing mine in return as if to comfort me.

"That man was cruel. He trained me to be a killer. If I missed a hit, if I hesitated—" I pause, jaw clenching. "I went to bed hungry. Or beaten. Sometimes both."

Her eyes flood with tears.

I hate it.

I love it.

Her pain, her empathy, it's a sickness in my veins. Something I crave. Something I never knew I needed until she came along and showed me what it was like to be completely enamored by a person.

Her fingers tremble before she lifts them to my face. Soft. Careful. Reverent. She traces the scar across my cheek, and I nearly stop breathing.

"Is that how you got this?" she whispers.

"It was when I refused a hit."

"What happened?"

"I killed him," I say. "And I escaped."

She blanches. Fear.

No. Please, no.

"Don't look at me like that," I beg. "I would never hurt you. Never."

Her eyes dart across my face, searching for truth.

"I worship you," I whisper. "I would burn the world for you. Do you understand?"

She nods slowly, but it's not enough.

I see the way her gaze flickers back to my scar.

"It disgusts you?" I murmur, and it kills me how raw my voice sounds.

"What?"

"I promise I'll treat you so well, you won't even notice the scar is there anymore. No man with perfect skin would ever treat you the way I treat you."

That thing on my face is gnarly. It's scared kids I've walked past on numerous occasions. I never cared. But the thought that it disgusts her makes me feel sick.

Is that why she won't kiss me?

"I like it," she whispers.

A slow, wicked grin spreads across my lips.

"You like it," I echo.

She presses her lips together, refusing to repeat herself.

"Then you like me," I tease.

For the first time, she doesn't deny it.

Chapter Fourteen
Amelia

I sit in the passenger seat, hands resting over my too-full stomach, eyes heavy with the kind of sleep that creeps in after warmth, sugar, and laughter. That was the best date of my life. Not that I have anything to compare it to. Still, I don't think anything could beat this.

The car slows to a stop. I reach for the handle, but a soft *tsk* pulls my hand back. Before I can blink, he's already out. He opens my door, his hand extended. My monster is a gentleman in the light, but we both know we live in nothing but darkness. I take his hand.

I step out, wobbling slightly. His hand catches my waist.

"Careful," he says.

We walk side by side. I don't even bother pretending I think he's leaving after this. He hasn't missed a single night since I arrived. Not one.

Inside the restaurant, it's quiet. Just us and the hum of the refrigerator compressors. I walk toward the back, and he follows. I kick off my heels, sighing in relief, and stretch my arms toward the ceiling.

"Full?" he asks behind me.

"Stuffed," I say with a small laugh, turning to face him. "You didn't need to order dessert too. You're trying to kill me."

He shrugs. "I like to spoil you."

My chest warms. What is wrong with me? This man confessed to having been a hitman, a person who killed and earned money from it at some point. Yet, here I am, absolutely swooning over his every word.

I lower myself to the edge of the bed and start pulling my hair out of its braid. He watches, just like a predator caught mid-hunt but fascinated by the stillness.

"You can't sleep here forever," he grumbles.

"It's not forever," I say, combing my fingers through tangled strands. "Just until I figure things out."

"Or until I give you something better."

"What does that mean?"

He doesn't answer, and I choose to move on from the subject.

"You're always here," I whisper. "Do you ever go home?"

He pushes off the doorframe slowly and crosses the room. Closer. Closer still.

"This is home," he says. "Wherever you are."

My pulse stumbles. "That's—" I start, but the words evaporate. Too much. Too fast. Too dark. And I'm starting to hate how precious that makes me feel.

Silence stretches between us, but it's not empty. It's loaded with everything we're not saying; things I'm not ready to admit.

I hear him move. Just one step back. A mercy.

"Sleep," he says. "I'll be here."

He always is. Even when I don't see him, or when I wish I didn't feel safer because of it.

I lie down, facing the wall, and he doesn't say goodnight. The lights go off with a click, and the shadows crawl in. Stillness. Quiet. Him. And something inside me splinters open at the realization that I stopped being afraid of the dark the moment he stepped into it. But even in this darkness, I feel that he is watching me. I've become attuned to him.

"You're staring," I accuse, eyes closed.

"I can't help it. I'm always thinking," he confesses. "About you."

I snort. "That's not creepy at all."

He doesn't laugh, because for him, it's not meant to be funny…it's a confession.

"Alright, stalker. What are you thinking now?"

"I'm wondering how you ended up here. Alone. In a back room that smells like damp cardboard and tomatoes."

I don't know why I feel comfortable enough to spill my darkest secrets and my biggest sin. Maybe it's because he opened up to me. I have no idea, but I give in to this urge to expose myself to this man.

"They were going to burn me," I say softly.

Silence. A beat. Then—

"What?" The word slices the air.

Something in the room shifts, like the pressure has changed. Like the walls are holding their breath.

"They picked me," I continue. "The cult. My village. Whatever you want to call it. Every five years, they choose a girl. A virgin. A sacrifice to the creature of rot and fire." I let out a breathless laugh. "They told me I'd be a blessing."

He still hasn't spoken.

"I ran that night. Didn't stop running until I arrived here, and Margaret kindly gave me an opportunity to live."

Still nothing.

I finally muster the courage to look at him. His jaw is clenched so tight it looks painful. His eyes, black and bottomless, burn with something that makes my stomach drop.

He breathes out hard, pacing a slow circle. "They chose you. Dragged your name through those filthy prayers like they owned you."

"I don't belong to them," I whisper.

"No," he snarls. "You belong to me."

I'm starting to get used to him saying I'm his. That I actually belong somewhere—to someone. And that is dangerous.

"I should go there and burn the lies out of their throats. Smash the bones they kneel on," he growls like a caged beast.

I place a hand on his chest to calm him down. "I don't want to think about them anymore. I want to leave them in the past, where they belong. I want to live. I want to try the weird food carts on the street, and dance like the girls in the movies do, and sit in a shitty park and let the sun touch my skin."

His rage is quiet, but it crackles under his skin like a live wire. Yet he looks like he wants to push all of this violence he's feeling down... for me.

He pulls out his phone and scrolls through it. A song starts to play, slipping into the air like smoke.

"Dance with me."

"What?"

"You said you want to live. Let's start here."

My heart is a drum, and his voice is a match. I take his hand.

His palm is rough, warm. His hand settles against my lower back, the other gripping mine. We move slow, swaying more than dancing, but his body is all heat and tension and hunger pressed against mine.

"You never got this, did you?" he murmurs into my ear.

I shake my head. "No one ever looked at me like I was anything more than a vessel."

"I'm not them," he hisses.

The music curls around us, and his lips brush the side of my head.

"I don't know what this is between us," I say honestly.

"It's whatever you want it to be. For now, it's just this."

The song loops. I yawn without meaning to. He carries me to the bed, tucking me in like my mother used to. I watch him settle on the hard ground, propping his head against the wall, ready to sleep on the floor like he always does.

"Don't sleep down there," I catch myself saying. What am I doing? Am I really inviting my stalker into my bed?

But he isn't just my stalker, is he? He's the man who spoils me, who protects me, who makes sure no one disrespects me. How can I stop myself from craving him instead of fearing him, when he shows me more care than anyone else in my life?

I pat the mattress beside me. He hesitates for a second. Just one. Then he almost teleports to the bed with how quickly he jumps in. I bite my lip to stop myself from laughing.

Tonight, I officially invited my monster into my bed. I regret nothing.

Chapter Fifteen
Amelia

I think I'm in love with a hitman.

Is he still a hitman? I don't know. But that doesn't change the fact that he was, at some point. Not by his own free will, but still. What is my life turning into?

It was simpler in my small village, where even if there was a villain, everyone knew to stay away. The villain was dangerous. Unlovable.

Here?

I'm falling in love with the villain. A man with blood on his hands. A man who stalks me, suffocates me, worships me. The same man who handed me his credit card with a smirk and said, *Shop until you drop, little flower. And if you do, I'll carry you home.*

The worst part? I can't resist anymore.

Damien is withering away every sense of reason telling me this is wrong. That I'll end up hurt. That I should run while I still can. Instead, I'm standing in the middle of a boutique where a single dress costs more than my paycheck. I'm trying on luxury, slipping into indulgence, sinking into a world I don't belong to; but one Damien is dragging me into, whether I like it or not.

"Oh."

The sound is thick with condescension, and it comes from the same woman I met that day at the restaurant. She was bad then, she's worse now.

She looks so perfect it makes me want to throw something at her. But she's sneering at me like she's waiting for me to explain myself, as if I need permission to be here.

"I didn't expect to see you here," she mutters.

I give her the same once-over. "Neither did I."

She smiles, the kind of smile people sharpen their knives behind. "Shopping here? You must've taken a wrong turn. Or are you just... browsing?"

"Why? You work here?"

Putting people down isn't my thing, and I thought it would never be my thing. Yet here I am, matching her energy.

Her lips press together like she didn't expect I'd fire back at her.

"I'm Linda," she hisses, like giving me her name is a privilege I should bask in.

"Amelia," I whisper. Damn me, I really struggle with assertiveness. "Nice to meet you, Linda."

"So, Amelia," she purrs, eyeing the dresses in my hand, "who's paying for all this?"

Everything clicks. No woman is this cruel to another unless it's about a man. My hunch? This girl has her eyes set on Damien. Nothing else would make sense. I was polite to her that day at the restaurant, sweet, even. This hatred, this viciousness, it has to be because she thinks I'm trampling over something that belongs to her.

I keep my face impassive. "Who do you think?"

"Sweetheart, I think we both know exactly what he's doing."

Fire licks at my veins. "Do we?"

"Damien," she says, testing my reaction. "He gets bored easily, you know. Boys will be boys. He's playing with you now, but eventually, he'll come back to where he belongs."

Inside, something tightens. It tightens and tightens and tightens until I feel like I need to gasp for air. I hate that for a split second, doubt curls in my stomach. But I don't let it show.

"If that's true, why are you here, Linda?"

She gapes at me.

"If Damien always comes back to you, why are you chasing me down?" I let out a laugh, though this crap isn't comical at all.

"You sure seem awfully worried about me."

"Maybe," I continue, "it's because while you're here trying to get under my skin, Damien has been busy—taking me to dinner, buying me gifts, wrapping his hands around me—" I stop myself with a small, amused hum, like I've just remembered where we are. "Oops. Never mind."

I've never been—dare I say—a bitch. Yet here I am...

Her jaw clenches. Her face and ears turn red, and she looks like she wants to lunge at me.

"You think you're special?" She leans in so close I can smell her expensive perfume. "Do you know that man killed for me?"

What?

My monster killed for *her*?

"Damien brought me the head of the man who hurt me," she breathes, her voice dripping with satisfaction. "He's the kind of man who will do anything for the woman he loves. And *I* am that woman, no matter how much he strays."

I feel the blow land somewhere deep in my ribs. I want to be the only one who makes Damien that crazy. The only one who twists him up until he's on his knees for me. The only one he would kill for. I don't want this to be true. I don't want to believe she meant something to him. That she was once the woman who made him unravel. That the side of him I thought was only mine had belonged to someone else first.

"And yet, here you are. Fighting for scraps."

Linda goes rigid.

I turn to the cashier, who is actively pretending she hasn't been eavesdropping on our altercation.

 "I'll take all of these."

The card Damien gave me slides through the machine without hesitation. Linda's eyes burn into the side of my face, but I don't acknowledge her.

I meet her gaze one last time. "Enjoy your memories, Linda. It seems like that's all you have left."

I walk out, my heart pounding, fingers tight around the bags. Because no matter what I said, or how confident I tried to appear, I still felt like crying.

My heels slam against the pavement. I'm fueled by pure rage. I don't think I've ever been this angry. Ever. Linda's words replay in my head like a broken record.

He killed for me.

Damien brought me the head of the man who hurt me.

Of course he did. Of course Damien was once unhinged like that for someone else too. I hate how it burns.

The soft purr of an engine glides beside me. A sleek black Porsche keeps pace with me like it has all the time in the world. Like I don't exist outside of it. I already know who it is without even having to look.

The window rolls down. "Get in."

His voice. Deep. Velvety. It still pulls me in, despite how badly I want to kill him right now.

I keep walking. "No."

Damien takes off his sunglasses, revealing the piercing blue eyes I refuse to meet.

"I see my little flower wants to be disobedient."

He parks.

Oh, hell no.

I start running, but the bastard is faster. One second I'm storming away, and the next, I'm airborne.

"Damien!" I shriek as he throws me over his shoulder.

"Mm." His grip tightens around my thighs as he strides back to the car. "That little attitude of yours is fucking adorable."

He tosses the bags into the backseat before shoving me inside.

"You can't manhandle me."

"Watch me."

He's so annoying.

"Now, tell me what's wrong with you," he grunts.

I fold my arms across my chest. "You're a liar."

"I've never lied to you. And I never will." His voice is softer now, but there's steel underneath it. "Tell me what's got you so angry. Let me prove to you that your man will never displease you."

I suck in a breath, my resolve teetering. But the jealousy surges again.

"You told me I was the only woman you ever chased. The only one you were obsessed with."

"You are."

"Well, that's interesting, because I just had a very enlightening conversation with a woman who thinks otherwise."

"Who?" That singular word comes out of his mouth like a death sentence.

"Linda." I nearly spit her name. "She told me you killed for her."

A muscle in his jaw ticks. "That bitch."

"Seriously?"

"Don't believe a word she said."

I shake my head. "Did. You. Kill. For. Her?"

"I did."

I reach for the door handle, but Damien is faster. He grabs my wrist and yanks me over until I'm straddling his thighs, his arms locking me in place. His scent invades my senses, cologne, leather, and something purely him.

"It was a job. A hit her father paid me for," he growls. "She was nothing. It meant nothing."

Maybe I should've realized, the moment I felt relief over the fact that he killed because it was business, not love, that it was the moment I lost my mind.

At that instant, I didn't care that Damien kills people for money. All I cared about was that he didn't kill because he loved *Linda*.

My nails dig into his shoulders, frustration boiling over.

"But me? You obsess over me?"

His grip tightens, his fingers bruising against my waist.

"I'd kill someone for just looking at you wrong."

His voice drops lower, rough with something almost feral.

"And if that bitch wasn't a woman, she wouldn't be breathing right now."

His words settle into my bones. Violent. Possessive. Unshaken. I believe him. But it doesn't erase the jealousy clawing through my veins.

I glower at him. *Mine. Mine. Mine.*

"Still angry, little flower?"

I don't answer.

"Mark me. Claim me. Make sure everyone I interact with knows I belong to you."

The challenge is too tempting. Before I can think, I grab his hair and pull his head back. I sink my teeth into his neck. Hard. Again. Harder. My lips trace fire down his throat, my teeth leaving bruises in their wake. A bite. A kiss. Another mark. And another. Until his neck is littered with evidence of me.

His hands fist in my dress, his breathing ragged. "Fuck."

I pull back, my lips tingling. Damien's pupils are blown wide, his expression wrecked.

"Mine," I whisper.

"Say it again."

I graze my teeth over his jaw. "Mine."

Damien grabs my hand and places it over his heart.

"No one makes me feel like this but you." His lips ghost over my ear. "And no one ever will."

Chapter Sixteen
Damien

My obsession. The bane of my existence. My reason for breathing, for existing... for living.

She's straddling my thighs, marking me with her mouth. Each hickey sears through my skin and straight into my fucking soul. My little flower, staking her claim, pressing her lips into my flesh like she's carving herself into me. And she is. She already has. She's in my blood, in my bones, in every breath I take.

Have I died? Is this heaven? Or is it some cruel hallucination—where I finally have what I want, but in the end, it's just an illusion?

Because nothing has ever felt better than this.

But something festers beneath the pleasure. Something dark. Possessive. I love seeing her riled up, jealous, her touch desperate and needy. But I fucking hate that she had any reason to feel this way. She should never doubt where I belong. Who I belong to.

Her. Only her.

I've failed if she even had a second of insecurity.

Linda. That little parasite latched onto my life the moment I turned her down. Entitled. Pathetic. But now? Now she's stepped into territory she has no business being in. She tried to put doubt in my flower's mind. Tried to wedge herself between us.

She won't get away with it. I'll make sure of that.

Amelia pulls her mouth from my neck, her lips red and swollen. I feel her gaze peeling me open. Unconsciously, I turn my head, angling my face away.

Her fingers catch my jaw, forcing me to look at her. I've never hidden from anyone, never cared how anyone saw me. But her...

She's staring at my lips like she wants to devour me, the same way I want to devour her.

I trace the swollen curve of her bottom lip. "I bet you've been wondering, haven't you?" I rasp. "Why I tasted every delicious inch of you but not these lips."

"Don't ruin the moment," she whispers.

I let out a dark laugh. "I wanted you to choose, little flower. I wanted you to decide if you wanted to kiss a beast of a man." My thumb brushes her cheek. "I know my scar isn't exactly—"

Something shifts in her expression. Something haunted. Broken. And fuck, I want to rip my own tongue out for whatever I said that made her look like that. Before I can say anything else, she crashes her lips into mine.

It's forceful, almost clumsy, her lips just pressing to mine, unmoving. She doesn't know how to kiss. It reminds me that I'm the first man to have this, to have her, in every way.

I take control, tilting my head, coaxing her lips open with mine, slowing her down, teaching her. My hands fist in her hair, keeping her where I need her. Her hands shake as they press against my chest, and I groan into her mouth, fucking obsessed with the way she melts for me.

When she pulls away, my breath is ragged, my restraint shredded.

And then she does something that destroys me.

She presses her lips to my scar. Kissing it.

My body locks up. My pulse stops. My whole world tilts sideways. The instinct to push her off, to turn away, is overwhelming. I've never been insecure about this scar, never gave a damn what anyone thought about it. But with her? With the most beautiful woman I've ever fucking seen?

I feel exposed. Raw. Like she deserves something better. Too bad for her. I'm the only man she'll ever have.

I cradle her face in my hands. "You're so sweet," I whisper, breathing her in. "My little flower is so sweet."

And she is. Too damn sweet for the likes of me. Too soft, too pure, and I should feel guilt for wanting to stain her with my touch; but I don't.

I place her in the passenger seat, watching the way she pouts. "If you keep touching me like that, I won't be able to control myself anymore," I murmur. "And I'm not taking your virginity in a car."

Her entire face turns scarlet, and I chuckle, gripping the wheel tight as I start the drive back to the restaurant. The sexual tension in the car is suffocating.

Not in a car, I remind myself. *Not in that shitty storage room either.*

She's coming home with me. And when I finally take her, she'll see fucking stars. And then, when I have her exactly where I want her, I'll convince her to stay.

When we arrive at the restaurant, she fumbles with the keys, hands shaking slightly. I take them from her.

"Let me." I unlock the door, and the moment it clicks shut behind us, I have her pinned against it.

My mouth crashes against hers, and she melts.

Soft. So fucking soft. She tastes like honey, warm and addicting, and just as I deepen the kiss, there's a pounding on the door.

Fuck.

I already know who it is.

Linda.

I should've known she wouldn't let this go. My fists tighten at my sides. If only my morals allowed me to kill her, this would be over. But I made a vow to myself the moment I escaped the man who pulled me into this world—a man so fucking insignificant now that I won't even waste my breath saying his name.

After I ran, killing was all I knew. I tried to pull away. Took a shitty mechanic job. Barely scraped by. But then they found me; the people I used to do hits for. And they were convincing.

I gave in. But on my terms. No women. No innocents. No one forced into the life like I was.

Richard was one of the men who sought me out. Offered me six figures for a single hit. One of my oldest clients. But if his daughter keeps this shit up, I'll throw him away without a second thought.

The pounding grows louder.

"Damien!" Linda screams, her voice laced with hysteria. "Open this damn door! I know you want me. She's nothing compared to me. I have everything she doesn't! What does she have that I don't?!"

I don't want to let her in. I don't want Amelia anywhere near her. But I need to put a stop to this.

I rip open the door, and Linda nearly stumbles inside. She's disheveled, her pupils blown wide with desperation.

"The only one I want is the woman standing right behind me."

I don't give her time to speak before I rip my car keys from my pocket and hurl them to the ground at her feet.

"Get in the car," I command.

She smiles. A slow, sick, Cheshire grin. It's like she didn't hear anything I said before *get in the car*.

Sick, sick woman.

I see it in her eyes; she thinks she's won. That something is going to happen between us in that car. Pathetic.

She scrambles for the keys, rushes to my car, and starts the engine. It's like she's a dog trained to obey.

I turn back to Amelia. She's glaring at me, arms crossed, jaw tight. I grab her face, kissing her again, this time right in front of Linda, making damn sure she knows exactly where I stand.

"Don't get any crazy ideas in your pretty little head," I murmur against her lips. "I want you. Only you. I'm going to return Linda to her father and have her put in her place."

Her glare softens slightly. "I don't like it," she admits. "She's in your car. In your space. Alone. What if—"

"Don't." My voice is a growl. "Don't even finish that fucking sentence." I cage her in, pressing her back against the door again. "Even the thought of another woman putting her hands on me fills me with rage. No one touches me but you. No one touches you but me."

My chest tightens at how sweet she looks, even when she's mad.

"Pack a bag," I order. "You're coming home with me after this; I'm going to show you just how much I belong to you."

With one last peck on her lips, I head to my car. The second I get inside, Linda reaches for me.

I snap.

My fingers coil around her wrist like a vice. Violently, I shove her off.

"Try that again, and I'll break every last delusion in your fucked-up head," I threaten. "You don't touch me. You don't even breathe in my direction."

Linda startles but quickly recovers. "You wouldn't have let me in your car if you didn't want me here."

"The only reason you're in my car is because you wouldn't have walked on your own two feet where I'm taking you."

"What does she have that I don't?" she wails. "I could give you so much more, Damien. Power, wealth, anything you want. She's just a naive little girl."

I slam the brakes. The tires screech, the force jerking her forward.

My head slowly turns to her, and whatever she sees in my expression drains the color from her face.

"Say one more word about her. Fucking try it," I dare her.

She presses herself against the seat, suddenly aware of the monster she's been trying to tempt. But she's too far gone to back off now. She recovers, shaking her head.

"You think she's different? That she's pure? She'll ruin you, Damien. She doesn't understand us."

"There is no *us*," I snarl. "And the only thing ruining me right now is your fucking voice."

For the first time since this whole ordeal started, she finally looks scared.

Good. She should be.

I press the gas, taking a sharp turn. When she recognizes where we are, the blood drains from her face completely.

"No," she screams. "You wouldn't."

I don't answer. I just drive.

When we pull up, she tries to bolt. I grab her arm before she can, dragging her out of the car. She fights, but it's pathetic. I'm disgusted by her desperation, by the way she still thinks this will end any other way.

I throw her forward, shoving her through the doors.

The men inside barely glance up as I toss her like garbage in front of Richard.

Richard doesn't say a word. Just eyes his daughter, who is sprawled on the floor, shaking.

"Your daughter's been following me around like a damn leech," I say flatly. "No matter how many times I tell her no, she refuses to listen. I don't have patience for this shit, Richard. If she comes near me again, our business is done."

His face darkens. He looks at Linda with barely concealed rage. I can see the wheels turning in his head. He loves his daughter; never tells her no, but not enough to risk everything he's built. Not enough to risk me not being on his team. My skills are the best money can offer; I eliminate men most are scared to even utter the names of. Me not taking his hits means a loss of power.

"Linda," he bellows. "Is this true?"

"Daddy, please—"

He slams his whiskey glass down. "I asked you a question."

Tears spill down her cheeks. "I love him, Daddy. I love him! He's meant to be with me, not her."

"Enough."

He exhales slowly, then looks at me.

"Consider it handled, Damien. This will never happen again."

Linda sobs. "Please, no, don't do this. I'll stop, I swear. I won't go near him again."

"You had your chance, girl."

Richard gestures to one of his men, who steps forward.

"Make the call."

"No!" she gasps, clawing at the floor. "Daddy, please, not him! Anyone but him!"

But it's too late. The phone call is made, and within minutes, her fate is sealed.

An arranged marriage. The man on the other end of the call is eager, and I can hear his excitement through the speaker.

She collapses, crying hysterically, but I don't give a fuck.

I turn to walk away, but not before delivering one last blow.

"Linda, if there's a next time, I won't be so merciful."

Chapter Seventeen
Amelia

I pace back and forth. I've paced so much it feels like my feet are going to fall off, but I can't stop. My thoughts are too loud, my emotions too raw. That woman is so pretty, even though she's rotting on the inside. And she's in an enclosed space with Damien.

My Damien.

The thought comes unbidden, like an instinct that's always been there. When did I start thinking of him as mine? When did the lines between fear and love blur into something I can't untangle? Maybe it was when he let me see the parts of himself no one else had ever touched. Maybe it was when he peeled back his skin and let me glimpse the bleeding heart beneath it.

I still can't believe this powerful, terrifying man was once beaten and left to starve. It makes me sick to my stomach. I hate the thought of what he suffered, of what was stolen from him.

He killed the man who did that to him.

Good.

God, what's become of me? If my mother heard me right now, if she knew the kind of thoughts swirling in my head, she'd think I was cursed. Possessed. She'd shun me like the rest of the village. But is everything really that black and white?

My phone rings, slicing through my thoughts. I jump and fumble for it. Ruby.

"Hey."

"Girl, are you okay?" Ruby's voice is clouded with concern. "Why weren't you answering my texts?"

I groan, rubbing my temple. "I'm really bad with messages, you know that."

"You're awful, Amelia. You stress me out. Anyway, what's up? Are you at work?"

"Uh, no, I'm... at home." I glance around the restaurant. It's the closest thing to home I've ever had.

"Perfect! I'm at that cute little café down the street from the restaurant. Can you come?"

I hesitate. I could stay here, stewing in my own thoughts, pacing until Damien returns. Or I could get out of my head and enjoy myself a little.

"Yeah, I can come."

"Great! Oh, but—" Ruby pauses. "My brother's with me. That cool?"

Her brother? What does it matter? I need a distraction. I need to be anywhere but here.

"No problem," I say.

"See you then!" she says excitedly.

On the way there, a flicker of movement catches my eye.

"Hey, little guys," I coo at the group of stray cats huddled together, already reaching into my purse.

I always carry cat food with me. As soon as I tear open the bag, more cats start appearing. One, two, three—*oh my God*—four.

Five.

Six?

Are they multiplying? Did I just summon an army?

I crouch down, pouring the food onto the pavement. "Okay, okay, everyone gets a turn. No shoving."

They pounce on it immediately. One with a torn ear rubs against my ankle.

"I'd take you all home if I could."

But I can't. I don't even have a home to myself. Maybe this is why I have such empathy for strays; I feel like a stray myself most days.

With a sigh, I leave the entire bag and keep walking.

***

I walk into the café, immediately spotting Ruby near the window. She's waving frantically.

I rush over, and she pulls me into a tight hug that I return with the same vigor.

"I missed you too," I laugh.

"Why do you disappear like that? I was so freaking worried about you."

"I'm so sorry," I say sheepishly, rubbing the back of my head. "I'm just... really bad with messages."

"You're lucky I love you."

"I know." I grin.

"This is my brother, Theo," she says, introducing the guy sitting next to her.

Theo stands, offering a polite smile.

"Hey," he says.

I shake his hand. "Nice to meet you."

"Theo's visiting for a few weeks," Ruby explains. "I figured, hey, we're all here, might as well introduce everyone."

I nod along, scanning the menu.

Ruby suddenly perks up. "Oh! Did you ever finish those romance books I recommended?"

I wince. "About that..."

"Amelia!"

"I got distracted!" I protest.

"With what?"

I open my mouth, then close it. Yeah, no way am I telling her that a jealous, raging man showed me he could get me off better than words on paper.

"Life," I say instead.

Ruby sighs dramatically. "She's hopeless."

Theo chuckles. "I mean, I kinda get it. I don't really read romance either."

Ruby gasps, clutching her chest. "Betrayal."

"You act like it's a crime." I grumble.

"It should be!" she declares. "But fine, maybe I can find something with romance and... I don't know, mystery? Suspense? We can all read it."

"That could work."

Theo shrugs. "If there's a solid plot, I'm in."

Ruby's face lights up. "There we go!"

I hum in acknowledgment, sipping my coffee. "So, Theo, what do you do?"

"Oh, he's—"

Theo cuts her off. "I work in security."

"That sounds interesting."

Theo nods. "It has its moments."

And just like that, the conversation flows easily. I let the rhythm of their voices soothe my mind.

"You know, Theo teaches me self-defense all the time. Maybe he could show you a thing or two? A girl can never be too safe."

"Yeah, if you ever want to learn—"

A voice cuts through the conversation like a blade.

"She won't need it."

Damien.

He's standing right behind me, his eyes locked onto me with a look so dark, it makes my pulse stutter. He's perfectly composed on the outside, but the air around him feels lethal. A beast, barely restrained.

Theo glances at him, then at me, his brows lifting slightly in question.

Ruby, on the other hand, gapes at Damien. "Uh, who is this?"

Damien doesn't give me a chance to answer.

"Her boyfriend. Damien," he says smoothly.

He lifts me from my chair like I weigh nothing and drops himself into my seat. Then he pulls me onto his lap. My hands press against his chest, but he doesn't even acknowledge it.

"You must be Ruby. Amelia's told me about you," Damien hums.

That's not true, though, I didn't tell him anything about her. But am I surprised he knows? No.

Ruby straightens. "All good things, I hope?"

His fingers trace small circles on my hip. "Of course."

His focus returns to Theo. Like a predator locking onto prey. "And you are?"

"Ruby's brother," Theo says, almost grumbling. These two don't seem like they're going to get along. "Didn't realize Amelia was seeing someone."

"She is," Damien hisses. "Very much so."

Damien's lips graze the shell of my ear, his voice low, meant only for me. "You're going to regret this, little flower."

"How did you find me?" I whisper back, swallowing hard.

He looks at me incredulously, but I don't miss the way his index finger taps the necklace around my neck. My brows furrow.

Then he presses a kiss to my neck. Right in front of them.

Ruby shifts in her seat. "Sooo, how did you guys meet?"

Damien drags his knuckles along my thigh; way too intimately for a public setting. "Fate."

Ruby gives me a look, clearly expecting me to elaborate.

"Uh," I manage, my voice unsteady. "We… met a while ago. At the restaurant."

It isn't a complete lie…

"She was meant to be mine," Damien murmurs. "From the moment I saw her."

Ruby watches, fascinated. Ever the romantic at heart, she transforms from skeptical to heart-eyed in seconds.

"You were talking about self-defense?" Damien growls at Theo. "That won't be necessary. Amelia is always under my protection."

"Still, it's a good skill to have. You can't always be around," Theo argues.

The temperature in the room drops.

"Can't I?" Damien chuckles.

Oh, he can. I know he can.

Theo doubles down. "Accidents happen."

"Not on my watch."

And I'm on his watch twenty-four seven.

Damien pins Theo with his glare again. "It's impressive that someone with your build can hold his own." A small pause. "Really, quite admirable."

That was mean. Theo is not small, it's just Damien that's much bigger than the rest of the male population.

Ruby coughs, interrupting the war brewing between the two men. "So! Who wants dessert?"

Damien clearly charmed her enough for her not to take offense at her brother being insulted. Hearts are shooting out of her beautiful brown eyes and aiming straight at us like some kind of cupid.

Traitor.

Chapter Eighteen
Damien

Jealousy.

It's the devil. A devil that crawls under my skin. I'm barely holding on.

Theo. Theo. Theo.

That little fucker.

My teeth grind at the memory of him looking at her, speaking to her, breathing her air. Anything my little flower needs, she gets from me. No other man provides for her. No other man teaches her a damn thing. That is my privilege. My right. My goddamn duty. I am her provider. Her protector. Her man. Her stalker. Her everything.

And she needs a lesson in that tonight.

I drag her out of the café the second that little meet-up wraps up. I don't slow down until we reach my car, parked in a secluded alley.

She yanks her wrist. "You're hurting me."

I let go, but only to cup her jaw and force her to meet my gaze. "You'll survive."

Fire flickers in those big, defiant eyes. "You're acting crazy."

I hum, dragging my thumb over her lower lip, my other hand settling on her hip. "Crazy for you, little flower."

I spin her, pinning her against the hood of my car, her palms slapping the metal.

"Did you pack a bag?"

"What?"

I nip at her earlobe. "Your bag, Amelia. Did you pack one like I told you?"

"No," she says slowly, testing the waters.

"That won't be an issue. I prefer you naked anyway."

She jolts, twisting under my grip. "What do you mean?"

"You know what I mean."

Her lips part. Eyes wide.

"I'm not taking your virginity in some dirty storage room."

Her face flushes crimson. She stammers, "What makes you think I still want you to take it after everything that happened? After Linda?"

She wants to pretend she doesn't want this? That she isn't mine? My palm cracks against her thigh.

She screeches, jerking against the hood. "What are you doing?"

Another slap. Harder. "What. Did. I. Tell. You?" I hiss. "Didn't I tell you the mere thought of another woman touching me fills me with pure rage?"

She turns her head, icing me out.

Wrong move.

I spread her thighs apart, stepping between them, pressing her down onto the hood.

"Whatever her name was didn't touch me."

Her eyes flicker with something like relief.

"She tried," I continue, pressing kisses along the column of her neck. "But I didn't let her."

"Why?"

"Because I belong to you. Body. Heart. Soul."

A shaky exhale escapes her lips. But it's not enough. That relief I should feel, it isn't there. Jealousy still gnaws at me.

"Are you being this difficult because of Theo?" I murmur. "Hmm? You saw him and now you want a taste of something normal? Something sweet?" I drag my lips along her jaw, voice dipping into a sneer. "A man who teaches you how to defend yourself instead of dismantling anyone who hurts you? If that's what you want, too bad. I'm the only man for you. You'll never get fucking normal. Only me."

"I don't want Theo," she huffs, but she's softening.

"I can't stand it, Amelia," I growl. "You leaving me. Hiding from me. Thinking I wouldn't find you. That I'd ever let you go. And for that, you're due for a punishment."

"Punishment?"

"Don't worry, little flower. I'll make sure you enjoy every second of it."

I kiss her in a way that leaves me starving. Not for air. Not for reason. For her. Always her. I tear myself away before I forget we're in public and strip her down right here on the hood, let the whole city watch me remind her who she belongs to.

No. That won't do. No one sees her like that but me.

I open the door and usher her inside. The ride is thick with something potent. Electric. My hands grip the wheel tighter than necessary, knuckles white as I watch her from the corner of my eye. She's clutching a shredded tissue, tearing it to pieces.

Nervous.

She shouldn't be. There's no need.

She is my priority. My reason. My fucking religion.

The only thing she should feel—

Is worshipped.

The moment we pull up to my building, her mouth parts in awe, head tilting back as she takes in the height of it.

"You like it?" I ask.

She nods, but I don't linger. She won't be remembering the building, anyway. She'll remember what I do to her inside it.

We step in. The elevator is empty, and the moment the doors slide shut, I pin her to the wall. My hands cage her in. My mouth crashes over hers. She gasps against my lips.

We're in our own little bubble. Just us.

The Hellkeeper

A chime cuts through the haze, and the doors slide open. She's dazed, and I fucking love it. Love that I can steal her breath. That I can make her forget everything but me.

I lead her inside. The second she crosses the threshold, her breath catches.

The space is dim, candles flicker in nearly every corner, and petals are scattered across the floor. I wanted her first time to be special. So, when I finished up with Linda, I came straight here and set this up.

I hold out my hand. She takes it.

She follows the trail to the bedroom, where more petals blanket the bed. The candlelight casts shadows along the walls, turning the space into something sacred.

I kiss her trembling fingers. Then, I step back.

I unbuckle my belt, letting it fall to the floor. My fingers move to the buttons of my shirt. The fabric slips from my shoulders. She stares, her eyes roaming over every ugly mark.

I catch her tear before it falls.

"Don't cry for me, little flower."

Her small hands trail over my skin, mapping each scar. That man spared nothing to teach me to be "perfect." Cigarettes, knives, belts—he marked me every time I said no or missed a hit. I want to hide.

But it's her.

My Amelia.

And she doesn't look away.

She whispers, "I'm glad you killed him."

Something dark coils in my gut. The words shouldn't affect me like this. But they do. They make my cock throb, sending heat pulsing through me.

Because she understands. Because she could crook her finger and I'd fall to my fucking knees. Because this woman, pure as snow, is glad I killed a man. Just because he hurt me.

She's innocence. I'm rot. And somehow, we fit.

I reach for the side zipper of her dress. She hesitates, arms wrapping around herself as if I haven't already claimed every part of her.

"No more hiding," I rasp. "You were made for me to see. For me to worship. Let me see all of you."

Always obedient when it matters, her arms drop. The dress pools at her feet. And for a moment, I forget how to fucking breathe.

She is absolute perfection.

My eyes drag over her perfect skin, the curve of her hips, her long legs. She's something celestial, and I'm the ravenous sinner lucky enough to touch her.

"You're so perfect," I sigh. "You unravel me." A kiss to her nose. "You make me weak." A kiss to her lips.

Then I trace a path down her throat. My teeth graze her collarbone. I nip at her flesh, soothe it with my tongue, kiss lower. I reach the valley between her breasts, and my hands slide behind her to unhook her bra. She stiffens, but I hush her with another kiss.

"You're mine to adore," I say. "Mine to cherish."

I claim her breasts—mouth, tongue, hands. She arches into me, breathless.

I press kisses along her ribs, then lower, down to her stomach. My teeth scrape lightly against her soft flesh. Her fingers tangle in my hair.

I continue downward, stopping at the panties still shielding her from me. I blow warm air over the damp fabric, savoring her shiver.

"Shy like last time?"

She shakes her head.

Good girl.

I peel the lace from her body and just look.

"Beautiful," I groan. "Too beautiful for this world."

Her chest rises in shallow breaths. I brush my lips against the inside of her thigh, then the other, inhaling the delicious scent of her pussy.

"Take what you want, little flower," I say.

Her hips rock shyly, but she's whimpering, frustrated that she's not getting what she needs.

"More," I urge.

I stick out my tongue, teasing her with its heat, its promise.

"No god, no culture, no voice in your head will ever make you feel dirty for this," I rasp. "You are a goddess.

My goddess. My queen. I kneel at your altar, Amelia, and I will worship you until you beg me to stop."

Her body shudders, nails digging into my scalp.

"Yes, little flower. Just like that. Take what you want. Because tonight, and every night after, I'm yours."

She grinds against my mouth, finding her rhythm. Watching her gain confidence is the hottest thing I've ever seen. I eat her like a man starved, like I'll die if I don't taste every drop of her pleasure.

"Damien... it feels so good."

The sound of her voice makes my cock ache, but this isn't about me. Not yet.

She breaks apart, her back arching. Only then do I rise, wiping my mouth with the back of my hand, my eyes locked on her dazed expression.

I throw her onto the bed.

She barely has time to process before I'm over her, pinning her down. I line my cock up with her soaked entrance, pausing to take her in, wide-eyed, trusting, willing.

"Tell me you want it."

She swallows, cheeks flushed. "I want it."

"Say it like you mean it."

"I want you."

"I'll be gentle," I promise.

I push in slowly, giving her time to adjust. Her nails dig into my back and I hiss, the mix of pain and pleasure perfect. She's crying softly at the stretch.

"It hurts... it burns, Damien."

"I've got you, little flower. Just breathe. Let me in."

She nods, body gradually relaxing. I don't move until she melts around me.

I try to be slow, to be gentle, but it's her. It's Amelia. And I lose control fast.

I take her hard. I worship her with every thrust, every moan, every bite I leave behind. This is devotion. This is what we were made for. When she finally shatters beneath me, body convulsing, voice hoarse from screaming my name, I follow. Deep. So deep I swear I become a part of her.

I pull out slowly, fingers trailing down her stomach, slipping between her legs. She jerks in overstimulation.

"Oh, little flower," I croon, sliding two fingers inside her.

"You disobeyed me," I remind her as she squirms. "Did you think I'd let that slide?"

I curl them inside her, dragging against her sweet spot. She wails.

"Please... no. No more."

"No, no. You don't get to beg yet."

I lower my mouth to her, tongue finding her swollen, overstimulated cunt. She pleads, says she can't take anymore, and begs for a break.

I don't budge.

Not until she breaks again.

And again.

And again.

She's crying now. "Please," she sobs, "n-no more. I can't."

"Oh, little flower," I murmur, "You'll take whatever I give you… and you'll love every second of it."

Chapter Nineteen
Amelia

My eyes open to the feel of strong arms wrapped around me. I close them again and allow myself to bask in it, to feel the safety, the security. Pure bliss—before the thoughts come. The calm before the storm.

I test his grip, but his arms tighten around me like steel bands.

"Where do you think you're going?" His morning voice is enough to melt any woman alive.

"Bathroom," I whisper.

A low grunt, then his arms loosen just enough for me to slip away. I move fast before he changes his mind.

I finish my business. Then, stand in front of the mirror. My fingers trace my skin. My body no longer feels like mine. I did it. I finally lost the last thing that could have tethered me to my old life.

I broke every rule. I am a sinner now.

But God, does sin feel good. Damien makes it feel like heaven. How can something meant to damn me feel like salvation? How is that fair? I tell myself I don't believe in the things my village preaches. I tell myself I don't believe in their God. That I am not religious. But does that stop the guilt? No. No matter how much I try, I can't look at myself without seeing someone who is ruined.

Damien materializes behind me in the mirror, a dark shadow swallowing the light. For a long moment, we just stare. He, at me. I, at him.

I take the time to admire the differences I definitely felt last night. He is tall, so much taller than me. My head barely reaches his shoulder. While my skin is soft and smooth, his is scarred and tattooed. Where I am soft, he is nothing but muscle. Darkness and light. Predator and prey.

He kisses my shoulder. I let him touch me, own me, possess me with just a press of his lips.

I look down, and it's as if I only now realize I'm naked. That shyness? That fear? It's gone. It evaporated into the steam curling from the bath he's drawing.

He turns the water off and holds out his hand. "Come."

I take it, and he leads me into the water. He sinks into the tub first, pulling me in after him until my back rests against his chest. I trace patterns on his damp skin, writing out all the things I feel inside.

"What's wrong?"

I hesitate. But this man has seen me naked. This man kissed me between the legs. What's left to hide?

"I feel dirty."

"Don't," he growls. "You feel me. That's what you feel. And I don't make you dirty. I make you mine."

He tips my chin up, so I have no choice but to meet his eyes. They are darker than before; nearly black. Consuming.

"Listen to me, little flower. Nothing will ever make you feel filthy for wanting this. For wanting me. They don't get to soil what belongs to me."

A breath catches in my throat.

"You think this is sin? Then let it be sin. I'll worship at your feet, damn myself over and over again just to taste you. You are not wrong for wanting this. You are not wrong for taking what's yours. Do you understand me?"

"But—"

"No but. There is nothing filthy about you and me. What we do together is sacred."

Something that feels a lot like salvation wrapped in destruction rakes over me at his words.

"You are my religion now. And I don't pray to anyone but you."

This man who breaks me apart then puts me back together in whatever way he pleases... and I let him.

Maybe I am ruined. But is that so bad?

I prop myself up, turning to face him. I trace over a scar carved into his chest; a jagged line that makes him flinch. Shame dulls his eyes.

"You can't tell me not to feel dirty," I whisper, my touch feather-light against his skin, "when you're ashamed of your scars."

His jaw clenches. A muscle ticks in his cheek.

"I'm not ashamed."

"Liar."

I lean in, pressing my lips to the raised mark. Then another. Then another.

"They're beautiful."

"You'll make me believe it one day, little flower."

Warmth spreads through my chest. But then, reality crashes in like a wrecking ball.

Work.

I jolt upright, slipping from his grasp. He watches, amused, as I frantically towel myself dry. I run to the bedroom. My bra is under the bed. Great. I retrieve it, snap it on, and then reach for the dress.

"Where are my panties?" I mutter, glancing around.

He's leaning against the doorframe, arms crossed, the very picture of smug male satisfaction.

"You won't need them."

I scowl. "Where are they?"

"Somewhere."

"Damien." My tone is accusatory.

"Amelia." He mimics the way I said his name.

I glare. He grins. But there's an edge to his amusement.

"Where are you going?"

"Work," I huff, running my fingers through my damp hair.

His smirk vanishes. "No."

"Yes."

"You don't need to lift a damn finger."

I cross my arms. "I like working at the restaurant. I love Margaret."

I can almost hear him counting in his head; anything for patience.

He exhales sharply, as if he's lost the fight. "Fine. For now."

"You don't get to decide when I quit."

His gaze snaps to mine, absolutely lethal. "I can and I will."

Before I can argue some more, he's moving. He stands behind me and begins dragging the bristles of a brush through my damp hair. My heart stumbles. No one has ever done this for me before.

"If you think for even a second that I'll let you sleep in that damn storage room any longer, you're dead wrong."

I close my eyes, biting my lip. He's impossible. Overbearing. Unhinged. But God help me, he makes me feel wanted in a way I never have before.

"We'll see."

"There will be no other option. I won't give you one."

I roll my eyes, ignoring the way my stomach flips at his words.

"I should leave."

"Wait." He rakes his hand through my hair one last time. "I'll drive you."

"Since when do you chauffeur me?"

"It's a perk that comes with you being mine."

I watch him get dressed, my gaze lingering far too long on the way his muscles shift beneath his inked skin. Heat pools low in my belly.

He notices. Of course, he does. His smirk is pure sin as he zips up his pants.

The drive is silent at first, but comfortable. Until he pulls into a flower shop.

"Are you getting in touch with your romantic side?"

He scoffs, shutting off the engine.

I follow him inside, observing as this big, scary man roams the shop. He picks up a bouquet of deep red roses, handing them to me.

I take them, trying not to swoon. He grabs another bouquet filled with soft pink lilies and white tulips.

"Who's that for?"

"Margaret."

I gape at him. "You like Margaret?"

He shrugs and hands the florist his card. "She took my girl in."

His girl.

"Margaret is going to think you have a crush on her," I tease.

"Anything to get me extra points with you."

This man is perfect, if you overlook the fact that he's a stalker and a hitman.

Back in the car, I hug the bouquet closer to my chest.

"You're going to be the death of me," he murmurs, almost to himself.

I snort. What did I do? Appreciate his gift? Is that so bad?

The rest of the drive is silent. But when he parks in front of the restaurant, nerves have me ready to babble; anything to stall going inside.

But I'm involved with an absolute bulldozer of a man, and he just grabs my wrist and drags me in.

I've never been this nervous to see Margaret before, but now the dark shadow that used to haunt me walks beside me, no longer hidden. He's here, in the light, for everyone to see.

Margaret stands behind the counter. Her brows lift when she sees Damien. Her gaze slides to me, curiosity blooming in her expression.

"Amelia," she says, "and…?"

"Margaret, this is Damien," I mumble.

Damien steps forward and offers her the bouquet. "It's a pleasure to finally meet you. Amelia speaks highly of you."

"Well, aren't you charming?" She takes the bouquet. "I didn't know Amelia had a boyfriend."

"She's full of surprises."

I try to change the subject. "I'm sorry I'm late."

"It's fine. Everything's handled," Margaret reassures me.

She leans in, whisper-yelling. "And, my dear, where have you been all night?"

Kill. Me. Now.

"Busy," Damien says, not even bothering to hide that he was eavesdropping. "With me."

Margaret giggles like a schoolgirl. "Oh, I like you. You make her blush."

"I should get to work," I blurt out.

"Of course, sweetheart," Margaret says, still grinning. "But Damien, you're welcome here anytime."

In a split second, everything changes. I think it's a reminder that people like us don't get happily ever afters.

Glass explodes. Screams rise.

The scent of roses is drowned out by something metallic.

Gunfire.

Chapter Twenty
Damien

Gunfire. Bullets. Rifles.

They've never scared me. I was raised between them, slept through the sound of them, killed with them. I've been in the middle of shootouts more times than I can count. But this time?

This time, there's fear.

For the first time in my life, real, gut-wrenching, soul-crushing fear grips me. Not for myself, I've never cared about my own life. But for her. The only thing in this godforsaken world that belongs to me. The only one I love. I would die for her. I would kill for her. I will rip the world apart for her.

"Get down!"

My voice is pure command as I shove Margaret under one of the tables, dragging her frail body further in. Amelia is beneath me, crushed under my weight, but I don't move. I don't give her space to breathe because if a bullet is coming, it will find me first. I press her into the ground, covering every inch of her, my body shielding hers like a living bulletproof vest.

She's shaking. My girl is scared.

"Breathe, baby. I've got you. I swear on everything that bleeds, I'll teach these fuckers what it means to put what's mine in danger."

The bullets keep flying, glass shattering around us.

Then silence.

I lift my head.

They're gone.

I push myself off Amelia instantly. My hands roam over her body, searching for any sign of blood.

"Tell me you're okay," I demand. "Tell me you're not hurt."

"I-I'm fine."

I need to see her eyes. Need to see for myself that she's not lying just to stop me from losing my mind.

But she looks over at Margaret first and pales.

She's lying in a pool of blood.

Amelia rushes to her side, pressing her hands to the wound on her stomach.

"Margaret, please, stay with me. Keep your eyes open, okay?"

I tear my gaze from Amelia; just for a second. The smell of gunpowder and death clings to the air. The restaurant is in chaos. People from nearby shops rush in, screaming, calling for help.

But a masked man outside catches my eye. He's dressed in all black, his hands trembling. A gun peeks from the waistband of his jeans.

One of them is still outside.

I grab Amelia's face and crush my mouth against hers in a brutal, claiming kiss. Then I growl, "Put pressure on her wound. I'll be back."

"Damien—don't—"

She wails as I pull away. But I don't stop.

Someone tried to take what's mine. And now? I'm going to take everything from him.

I break into a sprint, my blood boiling over. The bastard sees me. He fucking sees me and runs.

He bolts through the alley, his feet slamming against the pavement, but I'm faster. I was raised on blood and violence. Raised to hunt. Raised to kill.

He turns a corner. I turn with him.

He jumps over a fence. I scale it.

He makes the mistake of looking back.

I lunge.

I yank him back so hard he stumbles. Before he can recover, I slam him into the nearest wall. He groans. I don't give a fuck. I grab the back of his head and smash it again. And again. And again. Until he's barely conscious, slumping in my grip like a ragdoll.

Then I pull my gun, pressing the barrel to his forehead.

"You picked the wrong fucking man to pull this shit on," I growl, pressing harder. "You have two seconds to tell me who sent you before I paint this wall with your fucking brain."

His pupils are blown wide. He tries to form words, and I cock the gun.

"One."

His mouth opens.

"Two—"

I rip the mask from his face. That's when I realize I fucked up. It's a fucking ploy. A distraction.

This is one of Richard's men. I've seen him a shit ton of times. Which means Linda planned all this.

Linda that has her eyes set on my girl.

Fuck.

How could I have been so stupid? He was planted outside for a reason.

Linda wanted me to run. To leave.

Amelia.

My whole body goes cold.

I let go of him instantly, his body hitting the pavement like a sack of meat. I shoot him in the head. He doesn't matter anymore.

I turn and run back; faster than I've ever run before.

My lungs burn, my chest crushing in on itself, my vision going black around the edges. My gun is still in my hand, my fingers twitching around the trigger.

If I get back there and something happened to her—

If she's hurt—

If she's gone—

I will burn the whole world to nothing but ash.

I shove past the bodies crowding the restaurant.

"Amelia!"

My voice rips through the air, raw, desperate, unhinged.

 No answer.

I'm going fucking insane.

I spot Margaret on a stretcher. They're wheeling her toward the ambulance, her apron soaked in blood, her wrinkled hands shaking. But it's not the wound that has her face twisted in terror. It's something worse.

The second she sees me, she lunges, her bloody fingers grabbing my arm in an iron grip.

"Damien," she gasps. "Damien, they took her."

Everything inside me stills.

"You need to save her," she sobs, clenching onto me as the paramedics try to pull her away. She won't let go. She's fighting them with the little power she has left.

"She was screaming for you," Margaret cries. "Screaming for you, Damien." Her voice breaks. "They took her to Hell."

The paramedics yank her from me. The doors slam shut.

Hell.

I know where that is.

I'm already heading to my car.

The Hellkeeper

They think they took her.
They don't know—
 I'm bringing hell to them.

Chapter Twenty-One
Amelia

Hell follows me everywhere I go.

It burns the people I love just like it burns me. Maybe I was never meant to escape it.

I press my hands harder against Margaret's wound, my fingers slipping in her blood. The restaurant is chaos. Shouting. Wailing in the distance. People screaming. But all I hear is the faint, wet rasp of her breathing. It's way too shallow and slow. Margaret is old and fragile. I hope, with everything inside me, that she can survive this.

"Margaret," I choke out. "You have to hold on, okay? Just a little longer."

She blinks up at me, unfocused and delirious.

"I love you," I whisper, my voice breaking. "I don't think I ever told you that. But I do. I love you so much. You don't get to leave me, okay? You don't get to die before I show you how much you mean to me."

She smiles, and it shreds me.

Her thumb strokes my cheek. "Oh, my sweet girl," she murmurs.

Her hand is bloody, and her thumb smears the red liquid on my cheek. "I took you in because I understood you," she says softly. "Because I saw myself in you."

"Margaret—"

"I'm just like you," she cuts off whatever I meant to say. With a shaky breath, she confesses, "I ran too."

The world shifts beneath me.

Her nails bite into my skin. "I was supposed to be sacrifice number thirty."

I shake my head, horror creeping up my spine. "No," I whisper. "No, that's not possible."

The village never told us about any sacrifices escaping. It was a well-known fact: no one ever left the village. Ever. Not a single soul was born there and lived somewhere else. I thought I was the only one.

"Oh my god," I breathe, clutching at my heart, which feels like it might stop at any moment.

All this time... I was with someone who's just like me? Another sacrifice who escaped?

"You have to listen to me, Amelia," she begs. "This isn't right. They have something to do with this."

Her words turn my blood ice cold. The only thing keeping me sane at that moment is the sound of sirens wailing in the distance.

Margaret's state is deteriorating. She's sweating, and blood won't stop seeping out of her.

"Stay calm, Margaret. Help is on the way." I try to console her, but she seems to sense her end.

The Hellkeeper

The doors slam open, and two men storm inside. Masked. Massive. Rifles in their hands.

"Nobody move!" one of them bellows.

The restaurant is already on its knees, and panic sets in again. We thought it was over. Where is my Damien?

Their eyes find mine instantly, and I don't even get the chance to run.

A hand grips my hair and jerks me back so hard my spine cracks. I claw at them, but the second man moves in, lifting me clean off the ground.

"No—NO!" I thrash, kicking wildly, slamming my heels into their shins, their ribs, anywhere I can reach.

Margaret is screaming my name, trying to crawl after them, her hands gripping their feet like it can stop them. One of them slams his foot down on her hand, hard, and she passes out.

Oh god.

I fight harder. Harder.

"Damien! Damien, help!" I bellow. My monster. My shadow. My everything. He'll save me.

The first man grips my throat, cutting off my air. "Shut up."

I choke on my scream as they drag me outside. The street is full of people, but no one helps me.

A white truck is parked right at the curb. Back doors thrown open, it's waiting for me like a hungry mouth.

No.

The second man yanks a chain from his belt.

No. No, no, no—

Cold steel slams around my wrists, tightening until I gasp. The other end of the chain is bolted to the truck's interior. They shove me inside, and the doors close behind me. The lock clicks.

It's okay. It's okay. I try to calm myself, whispering again and again that Damien is coming. He won't leave me. But my doubts laugh at me.

It takes a moment to realize the giggles aren't just in my head. They're inside the truck too.

Linda...

She sits across from me, a sick jester smile stretched across her face.

"Well, well. Look at you."

Linda sighs dramatically, like she actually pities me.

"I always knew something was off about you, so I did a little digging." Her lips curl. "And guess what I found?"

I glare at her, my entire body trembling. I say nothing.

"You came from Hell."

She knows. This is the worst that could've happened.

"Tell me, Amelia... don't you think it's time you went back?"

I suck in a sharp breath.

"I made some friends from your little village. Turns out, they were more than happy to help me drag you back." She gestures vaguely. "Said something about a debt that needed to be paid."

Sacrifice.

They're taking me back to be sacrificed.

"You should've kept your head down. You should've never gotten close to Damien."

I flinch at his name. Is he really coming to save me? Did he leave me? Can anyone save me at this point?

"Poor Damien. He has no idea, does he? No idea that you're such a fucking weirdo."

"You don't know shit, Linda." My voice is raw, furious. "You think he'll let you walk away once they're done with me? That he won't kill you for what you've done?"

Uncertainty flickers in her eyes, but it's gone just as fast.

 "Maybe he'll finally love me. You know, with you being gone and all."

"Fuck. You."

She chuckles, crossing her legs like she's enjoying herself. She's way too calm for someone handing me over to a fate worse than death.

I press back against the cold metal wall, heart hammering. My throat tightens, my lungs feel too small. But I don't let her see it. I won't let her see how fucking terrified I am.

"Did you actually think you'd have a happy ending? You? The girl who was never supposed to make it out alive? You're a fucking joke."

She walks closer until she's right in my face.

"I promise you, sweetheart. He won't even be able to find your body when they're done."

She's the devil. She has to be, with the way she twists her words into sharp knives and throws them straight at my heart.

"Maybe he'll look for a while. Maybe he'll even cry over you. But in the end? He'll forget. And he'll find me right there to comfort him."

I can't bite my tongue any longer.

"Is that what this is about? You couldn't have him, so no one else could? That's pathetic, Linda."

Her nostrils flare.

Bingo.

I don't stop. I want her to break. I'm dead either way.

"You're fucking miserable. Nothing more than a daddy's girl with more money than you could ever spend. But all that money, and still you're unlovable."

I lean forward, spit the truth in her face.

"No matter what you do, or will ever do, Damien won't ever love you."

I bellow the last words. "And guess what, Linda. You aren't just taking me to my grave, you dug yours too."

I'm sure of it. If Damien can't save me, if this is my last day on earth, then it'll be Linda's too.

That does it.

Her face twists, and rage floods her eyes. She lunges.

Her hands clamp down on my face so tight I'm sure her fingerprints will be branded into my skin. "You fucking bitch."

But they made a mistake.

The chains are too long.

I swing my arm back and punch her in the face, so hard her head snaps to the side. The chain whips forward and slams into her forehead.

Linda screams, clutching her face as she topples backwards. Blood pours down her face, and a few seconds later, she's unconscious.

"Oops."

Chapter Twenty-Two
Amelia

I don't know how long it's been. Hours, maybe.

The truck rattles over the bumpy roads, making the chains bite harder into my wrists. My arms scream from being held in the same position for too long. Everything hurts. My legs, folded beneath me, have long since stopped tingling, they just ache, stiff and useless.

Across from me, Linda hasn't moved. Blood mats her hair, a dark trail running down her temple where the chain snapped back into her skull. I did that.

I press my lips together, swallowing the swell of nausea. I can't afford guilt. Not when she's the reason I'm in this goddamn truck, being dragged into what can only be described as a nightmare.

This woman, this sick, pathetic excuse of a person, took everything from me. My freedom. My future. My goddamn life. She would have watched me burn.

What I did to her was survival.

I'd beg if I thought it would help. I'd scream and claw at the partition separating me from the drivers if I thought it would change a damn thing.

But I know better.

I know what's waiting for me.

The truck jerks to a violent stop. I lurch forward, and the chains nearly rip my arms out of their sockets. It feels like my shoulders are being wrenched apart, like the bones in my wrists are grinding together.

I can't take this anymore.

A sob bursts out of me before I can stop it. I break.

I don't want to die.

I still haven't told Damien that I love him.

Please, please, please, Damien.

Save me.

Save me.

The truck doors creak open, daylight spilling in like a taunt. The air is cold, but the hands that grab me are colder.

The man clicks his tongue in disapproval when he sees an unconscious Linda.

"Untrained little thing." Fingers curl around the chains, tugging them sharply. "Don't worry. That'll be fixed soon enough."

A fresh wave of terror slams through me as I'm yanked out of the truck and I see every face I've ever known. Familiar faces. Faces I grew up with.

They're sitting around a roaring fire, waiting.

The men drag me forward easily. My body has gone limp. I have nothing left to fight with. They force me onto my knees, my bones jarring against the dirt.

The people look at me with rage, with disgust, with hate. At that moment, I know they don't just want me to die, they want me to suffer.

A hush falls over the village.

Elder Gideon steps forward.

His beard is long and gray, his withered face showing nothing but satisfaction. Beside him stands Elder Tobias, shorter, rounder, with a small, sick smirk on his face and eyes that gleam with pure evil.

Gideon raises his arms. "With this girl's return, we are granted an opportunity. An opportunity to right what was wronged."

A murmur ripples through the crowd; voices of agreement and praise.

Elder Tobias steps closer, crouching until he's at my level. He smells like damp wood and rotting fruit.

"With this girl back," he continues, "we can finally amend our sins to the Hellkeeper. He will have two sacrifices in one year. One was a girl pure and innocent as snow. And the other—" He grips my chin, forcing my head up. "A wretch who will serve as a warning. An example of what happens to those who run from their duty."

A cheer erupts.

They're celebrating my death.

I try to rip my face away, but Tobias tightens his grip.

"She ran," he sneers. "She abandoned her fate. Turned her back on all of you." He wrenches my head from side to side. "Tell me, does she look innocent?"

"No!" someone shouts, but he's too far back in the crowd for me to recognize who.

"She is filth," a man spits, the same man who taught me how to knead bread.

"She reeks of sin!" bellows the woman I used to help sew.

Bambi walks over to me, I used to fish with her at the lake. Her hand flies across my face so hard that my ears ring.

"You deserve this," she hisses. "You deserve every second of this."

The crowd follows her lead. They get closer and closer. Neva and Meredith, the same girls I used to train cattle with, sneer at me. Neva spits right in my face.

"You ran from your duty. From us. Like you were better than this village. Better than us," Meredith rages.

I can't speak. I can't say anything. I don't even have the energy left to open my mouth.

All of them form a circle around me, and I can't see anything but their shoes. And they have their revenge.

Someone punches me in the stomach so hard I spit out red. Hands tangle in my hair and yank with so much loathing that a few strands rip free from my scalp. Another kicks me right in the ribs.

"Nothing but a disgrace."

Please stop.

Rocks are being thrown at me by a girl who is surely on their list to be sacrificed soon. But she shows no solidarity or even fear, only hate.

More follow. A rock hits my thigh. Another strikes my ribs. My feet.

They want me dead before the sacrifice even begins.

I'm dizzy. I taste blood, and I'm drowning in it.

They're animals. Demons dressed as humans.

I close my eyes, trying to block it all out, trying to picture Damien's face, his touch, his voice. But all I see are monsters.

"Amelia."

I lift my head slowly. It's like I've called an angel into existence. She looks like one, with her braided hair and loose gown.

The crowd parts for her. She's come to save me.

"Mother," I rasp. "Please—"

She slaps me hard. I flinch, my body betraying me with a whimper.

The crowd laughs.

"I bore you," she growls, her nails leaving imprints on my bloody face. "I loved you. And this... this is how you repay me? By embarrassing me? By staining our family name?"

The Hellkeeper

I wish I could believe this isn't her. That this isn't real. But something in me always knew my mother would choose the village over me any day. And today, she did just that. She chose her religion, the scriptures, the village, and even the damned Hellkeeper over her own daughter.

She turns away, lifting her hands to the sky.

"I call upon the Hellkeeper," she chants, "to purify this wretch before her sacrifice."

The crowd echoes her words.

Purify. Purify. Purify.

My mother walks over to an iron pot suspended over the flames and reaches for the wooden handle. The two men holding me tighten their grip.

"Mother—"

The water tilts.

And then—

Agony.

The water isn't boiling yet, but it's hot enough to make a million needles prickle across my skin. I scream until my throat is raw, until my lungs beg for mercy. But there is none. These monsters know no mercy. I have never felt this much pain in my life.

Death would be more merciful. This is torture.

"She is purified!" my mother declares. "Let her now be made worthy."

I slump forward, trembling, dying.

I don't pray to the Hellkeeper.

I pray to Damien.

Please.

Please come.

Please burn them all.

"Step back." Elder Gideon stands at the edge of the fire, his hand raised, his presence alone enough to make them obey. All they ever do is obey; like sheep following monsters and calling them righteous.

"For generations, we have shielded you from the truth," Elder Tobias begins. "We never let you witness the sacrifices. Not because we were ashamed, but because we did not want fear to drive you to foolishness."

They listen, hanging on his every word.

"But tonight... tonight, you will watch." His eyes sweep over the gathered crowd, taking in their reactions. "Because of her, you must. She proved to you that no one can run from their fate."

The elders circle me like vultures, their robes whispering against the dirt as they chant.

"The Hellkeeper waits below.
The flames cleanse the wicked soul.
Blood will spill, fire will rise."

Their voices rise in unison, eyes rolling back like they are possessed.

"The lost will burn, the faithful remain.
The Hellkeeper's wrath will be tamed."

They circle me a few more times, chanting in tongues before falling silent.

Is this it? Is it over?

"Lift her up," Elder Gideon commands the men who dragged me here.

They move me toward the massive tree standing before the fire pit. My body fights even as my spirit fractures, but they force my arms above my head, lashing the chains tight to a thick branch. The heat licks at my feet. Too close.

They're going to dangle me. Hold me over the flames like a pig on a spit. Let me burn alive, slowly, so every girl in this village understands...this is the only fate.

There is no escape.

There is no mercy.

There is only fire.

Chapter Twenty-Three

Damien

I drive like a man possessed. Because I am.

The road blurs, trees melting into shadows. I can hear her. Feel her. Every scream. Every sob. It carves out my sanity, bleeds me dry. They're hurting her. My little flower. My angel. And I will make them pay.

I taste blood. My own. I've been grinding my teeth so hard my gums have split, the iron tang flooding my tongue. But I welcome the pain. It feeds me. Fuels me. Prepares me for what I'm about to do.

The moment I hear the chanting, I know I've arrived in Hell.

I abandon the car, shoving the door open so violently it nearly rips off its hinges. My boots hit the dirt, and I run. The scent of fire hangs thick in the air.

I see her. Chained. Suspended above the flames like an offering to a creature that doesn't exist.

This village has no idea what it just unleashed.

I shoot the masked man holding the chain in an instant, and he crumples like a ragdoll, his head erupting in a wet explosion of crimson. The second man barely has time to turn before I send a bullet straight between his eyes.

The crowd erupts in screams. People scatter, running like the vermin they are. But two older men stay, still trying to lower my little flower to complete the sacrifice.

"You cannot stop this," one of them bellows. "The sacrifice must be completed. We offer her to the Hellkeeper—"

He must have missed the demons in my eyes. I raise the gun and fire. The bullet drives straight through his open mouth.

The other scrambles to lower Amelia down, frantically pulling at the chains. I cross the distance in two strides, grab him by the throat, and slam him into the ground so hard his skull cracks against the packed dirt. The chanting dies in a strangled gurgle.

My hands shake as I unchain her, as I cradle her fragile, beaten body against mine.

"I'm here," I murmur. "I'm sorry, little flower. But I swear to you, I'll make them suffer for every second you were in pain."

She's crying. Weak. But alive.

"I knew you'd come," she whispers. "I knew it."

I brush her blood-matted hair from her face. "I'll take care of everything. Just rest."

I carry her to the car, tucking her inside before pressing my lips to hers. Gentle. Reverent. The only soft thing left in me. I turn back to the village with the cans of gasoline I fetched from the trunk.

The time for revenge has come. All one hundred and twenty-eight acres of this space will go up in flames. All one hundred and forty-nine people will burn today.

I move like a demon through this rotten village, gasoline in one hand, gun in the other. My heart pounds, breath ragged from pure fury, from the sheer, unrelenting need to watch them all burn.

I begin with the first cottage. The fuel sloshes against the dry wood, soaking into the cracks. The scent of gasoline chokes the night air. A man stumbles out, eyes wide with terror, coughing on the fumes. He barely gets a word out before I put a bullet between his eyes. His body crumples to the dirt, lifeless.

I keep moving. The crops, this village's lifeblood, I drench them in gasoline. The stench thickens, suffocating and intoxicating. A man rushes at me, trying to slap the can from my hand. I barely acknowledge him before shoving him back. There's so much rage inside me that my strength feels inhuman.

A group comes next, five or maybe six men. Desperate. Terrified. They think they can stop me. That they can save this place.

There is no saving them after what they did to Amelia.

I pull the trigger. One drops. Another staggers, clutching his gut, then collapses. The rest hesitate, their courage bleeding out. One turns to run, I shoot him in the back.

Cowards.

I strike a match and flick it into the gasoline-soaked field. The fire erupts, an orange beast devouring the crops, crawling up the fences, racing toward the cottages.

Screams.

Panicked voices cry out. Some order water, others plead to gods that never existed.

A woman shrieks as flames catch her dress. She spins, slapping at herself, until she falls. Another man hauls a bucket from the well, hands trembling so hard he spills most of it. I shoot him before he can throw a drop.

Some of them still try to put out the fire with the little resources they have, or dart into the woods like rats. But very few of them actually try to stop me, not that they'll succeed either way, but it shows just how cowardly they are. Nothing more than sheep who don't know what to do now that their elders have died. I cut them off, one by one, like a butcher picking his cuts. They've already made their choice. They chose to burn her. So now, I burn them all. No mercy.

I watch, expressionless, as figures crawl from the inferno, coughing, crying, begging. It doesn't matter.

I raise my gun.

Bang.

Bang.

Bang.

One by one, they drop.

Those who try to run, I shoot without hesitation. The others, too terrified to move, I push into the hell they created. I watch it all, unaffected by the blaze.

Smoke thickens the air, choking the sky, turning it into a blood-stained haze. I keep going. Keep hunting. Keep burning. Until there's nothing left but ashes and corpses.

And I stand there, watching it all.

This is what they deserve.

The smoke begins to get to me. My eyes sting, and a rough cough tears out of my throat. I leave the village square after making sure there's no hope left for any of them.

But then I see the white truck, the one they came in, with Linda trying to escape it. Without hesitation, I pour the rest of the fuel over the hood, drenching it until gasoline runs down the sides and pools beneath the tires.

I strike another match. Flick it into the gas-soaked engine block.

The fire erupts instantly. The truck ignites, a blaze roaring beneath the metal. Glass windows shatter from the heat.

The glass explodes in my face. Shards slice into my cheek, but I feel no pain. Only satisfaction.

Linda looks at me with pleading eyes, silently begging, but I just watch her burn. That's what she deserves for what she has done.

I leave before the fire spreads enough to trap me and make my way to the car, parked far enough to avoid the worst of it. Still, the heat licks at my back. The fire will spread, fast.

I slide into the driver's seat, ready to get Amelia out of here.

But before I can start the engine, her bloodied hand rests on mine.

She doesn't speak. She doesn't need to.

I understand.

She wants to watch. Just a little longer.

So I let her.

She isn't just mine, she is me. Cut her, and I bleed. Hurt her, and I become death itself. My love isn't gentle. It's all-consuming. If she cries, I will carve out the tongues that spoke against her. If she bleeds, I will drown the world in the blood of those who hurt her. There is no limit. No end. Only fire. Only ruin. Only the bodies I would stack at her feet just to keep her safe.

I would burn everything. Everyone. Until there is nothing left but her and me in the ashes.

Together, we witness the last embers of this wretched place die.

Together, we end it all.

Chapter Twenty-Four
Amelia

Damien pulls into a run-down motel on the drive back. It looks abandoned, falling apart even. I think he wants us to rest a little before the long drive home.

The receptionist freezes when she sees us approaching. Her eyes flick to me, noting that I look absolutely battered. I can see it in her face: she's deciding whether or not to call the cops. Any sane person would. But before she can, Damien slaps a wad of cash onto the desk. Big, thick bills that make her swallow her conscience. She slides over a key without another word, her gaze pinned to the counter. I know what she's thinking.

And she'd be right. I was kidnapped. Hurt. Tortured.

But not by the man standing beside me.

Never by the man standing beside me.

I shift on my feet, the raw skin burning with every step. Damien notices immediately and sweeps me into his arms. My body melts against him, and I breathe him in. Gunpowder. Smoke. Blood. Rage. Not even a trace of the scent that used to cling to him. He's nothing but war now. A war he waged for me.

The door to our room creaks open, and it's dimly lit. We step inside. Just the two of us. A woman who's survived Hell. And the man who burned it to the ground for her.

Damien kneels at my feet, and something inside me cracks. He's a beast, a demon, the most terrifying man I've ever met, but he kneels. For me.

I don't know who in that village stripped me of my shoes, but it doesn't matter. They're dead now. All of them. He lifts my foot, his hands shaking. He stares at the blisters with a haunted, anguished look on his face. And then he presses his lips to my feet, kissing them like he can take the pain into himself. He's breaking, unraveling, falling apart right in front of me.

It's not hygienic. It's reckless. But I don't tell him to stop. Because I know he's barely holding on, and I'd give him anything he needs at this moment. He's just as traumatized as me.

He brushes the hem of my dress and pulls it over my head. It leaves me in nothing but my bra and underwear. He carries me to the bathroom and sets me on the sink, his eyes frantically scanning every inch of me. His whole body is tight with rage. His eyes are crazed. There's no other term for it. Absolutely unhinged.

I glance down at myself, even though I don't need to. I feel every bruise, every burn. My feet are blistered, had he come any later, they would have been charred.

The flames only licked at them because he saved me. He came just in time.

My ribs are purple. The rocks they threw gravitated toward them more than anything else, but I don't think they're broken. Just bruised. My stomach is a sick blend of green, blue, and yellow, the colors of a dead thing rotting, thanks to the punch that now-dead man landed on me.

My hair is tangled, my scalp raw from where they dragged me. There's a wound above my eyebrow, and dried blood clings to the side of my face. And then there's my skin, as red as a lobster courtesy of my mother.

My mother.

It only just registers.

She's dead.

And I don't feel anything.

Before today, I would have mourned. But from the first slap, from her words, from her choosing a bunch of stupid stories over her own daughter, she was just like every single other person in that village to me.

I'm pulled from my thoughts by his breathing. It's getting worse, harsher, quicker. He's hyperventilating. Murder rolls off him.

When he finally speaks, his voice is hollow. "I want to go back."

"What?"

"I want to go back." His jaw flexes. His throat bobs. "I want to bring them back. I want to make them breathe again, just so I can kill them all over."

I should be horrified, tell him to calm down, tell him he's not thinking straight. But I don't. Because his words warm my heart.

This man has successfully dragged me into the filth with him, into the darkness, into evil. I'm as much of a villain as he is. But being a villain doesn't feel too bad with him by my side. I'm elbows deep in sin, and I don't ever want to leave.

His heart pounds against my hands.

"It's done," I whisper. "It's over."

"No." He shakes his head violently. "No one marks you but me." His trembling hands trace my skin. "You're mine. Your body, your skin, all mine." His forehead drops to my thigh. "And I let them touch you."

I caress his hair, trying to soothe the storm raging inside him. "You came," I murmur. "That's all that matters."

"Not soon enough," he chokes out. "Not before they put their fucking hands on you. Not before they hurt you. I should've killed them before they even thought about it."

I tug on his hair, pulling his head back so I can see his face. His eyes are wild, and he looks pale.

The Hellkeeper

I smile, just barely. "And what would you have done, hmm? Killed the whole village the moment I was born?"

His lips part, and he doesn't answer.

Because he's thinking about it.

My man is absolutely evil, a psycho, but he's mine.

He lowers himself further, pressing his lips to my feet again. I twitch at the contact, the blisters tender, but he doesn't stop. He kisses over every burn, every raw spot, and the heat of his mouth sears me more than the fire ever could.

He presses a kiss to my shin. My knee. My thigh.

My ribs, the bruises there.

My stomach, the ugly green and blue of it.

Every single inch of skin they marked, he reclaims.

I bite down on my lip, eyes stinging. "My skin won't be smooth anymore," I mumble. "Would you mind?"

His fingers grip my jaw, tilting my head back roughly, forcing my eyes to stay on his. His pupils are blown wide, his expression unreadable. His lips hover over mine, close enough that I feel the heat of his breath.

"Mind?" His voice is lethal, low and sharp. He thumbs over the dried blood on my cheek. "Your body is mine. Your scars are mine. Every single mark they left on you belongs to me now. You are beautiful, and you will always be beautiful." He kisses down my neck, over the angry red skin my mother left behind. "And if you ever say something like that again, I swear I'll make you look at yourself in every mirror until you see what I see."

I believe him, and my insecurity dies the second it came up.

"I should've taken you to a hospital," he rasps. "I should be taking you now, but I can't. I fucking can't."

I feel his desperation. His self-loathing.

"I'd shoot them," he whispers. "I'd shoot whoever even looked at you. I'm barely holding on to my sanity, little flower."

At the mention of the hospital, something in me seizes.

"No," I breathe. "Please." I'm pleading instantly. "I just want it to be the two of us for a while. Just us. Please."

I'm terrified. What if someone snatches me back up? The only person I trust right now is Damien.

"Are you okay?"

I nod, curling closer into him. "I'm okay. I just can't trust anyone but you right now. I don't want anyone touching me but you for a while." I sound weak, but I don't care.

"I won't let anyone near you," he vows. "Not now. Not ever."

He leads me to the shower but hesitates. I know he's overthinking everything he does, making sure it doesn't hurt me. He can never hurt me. Sure, he scares the shit out of me sometimes. Sure, the way he loves is unconventional, but there is no doubt in my mind that this man loves me. So, I raise my arms in surrender, giving him permission to do anything he wants to me.

He unclasps my bra, and it slips down my arms, falling to the tile floor. My panties are off next.

"I'm so fucking sorry," he breathes against my skin.

"It's not your fault."

"It is," he snaps. "I let them—" He cuts himself off with a sharp inhale. "I should've locked you away so no one could hurt you. So that you would always be mine."

"I'm still yours."

"Damn right you are." I hear him mutter under his breath before he starts the shower.

I want to laugh at his words, at his possessiveness, but the water stings.

A sharp burn against my raw skin, my blistered feet. I flinch, and the pressure behind my eyeballs increases. The pain makes me sway a little, but Damien is right there, supporting me completely.

"I know, little flower," he murmurs. "I know. Just hold on."

He's careful, slow as he washes me, untangling the knots in my hair, soothing my aching scalp. He drags the washcloth over me with such gentleness that it's just like a whisper.

No one has ever treated me like this.

Like I'm something precious.

He wraps the motel robe around me before sitting me on the bed.

He grabs the first aid kit and kneels in front of me once again, disinfecting and bandaging my wounds with such focus it's like I am the center of his universe. And maybe I am.

"I love you so much." He confesses.

A tear slips down my cheek. "The whole time they were hurting me… when I thought I was dying…" I choke out a breath. "My only regret was not telling you. I love you, Damien."

"I can't forgive myself," he murmurs.

"Then let me forgive you."

I see the sheer obsession in his icy blue eyes.

He's drowning in me. And he doesn't want to be saved.

Chapter Twenty-Five
Amelia

I walk like I never have before.

There's a shift in the way I move, a newfound confidence. Darkness clings to me like a second skin. Because I know, without a shadow of a doubt, that a man who promised to burn the world for me, and actually did, walks behind me.

He's an anchor.

A force that steadies me, strengthens me, lets me act like a girl who has finally been unchained.

There's no more village looming over my head. No more whispered threats. No more sick ideologies pressing down on me with the weight of a thousand suns. No more invisible chains. No more boundaries keeping me locked in a life I never chose.

In this cold, unforgiving city, I've been able to form my own community. I made a cocoon with the people who understand me, love me: Margaret, Ruby, Damien. Ruby was beside herself when she heard the news. She kept asking if I was okay, and if I needed anything. I never expected anyone to care so much for me. And I'm so grateful for the people that make me feel like I belong.

My man freed me.

But he didn't just free me; he freed someone else too. Someone I care about. Someone who's lived in fear, just like I did.

I sit by Margaret's hospital bed, holding her hand tightly, my thumb brushing the fragile bones of her knuckles. It's been a few days since everything went down. Since the world I once knew burned to ash.

The surgery was risky.

But she's still here.

She looks different. Older. The fear, the exhaustion, the years of hiding have worn her down.

But she's here.

She survived.

And yet, she hasn't opened her eyes.

My throat tightens. I reach out, caressing her grey hair.

I hold back my tears. "Margaret."

Like the past few days, she gives me nothing.

"It's over," I whisper. "It's really, really over."

I press my forehead against her arm. "Damien burned it all down," I breathe. "The village. The people. The ones who hurt us. They're dead. All of them. There's nothing left. They can't touch us anymore."

"Please, open your eyes," I beg.

Nothing.

The heart monitor beeps beside me, its steady rhythm doing nothing to soothe the storm inside me.

"Wake up, Margaret," I plead. "The world's waiting for you."

Tears fall without my permission. A hand settles on my shoulder, warm, familiar. Damien.

He hasn't left my side since that night. Since he carried me out of Hell and never looked back.

"She'll wake up," he says softly. "She's strong. Like you."

My hand finds his, clutching it.

He's here.

I'm here.

We're free.

"The nurse is waiting for you."

I stiffen. He notices instantly.

"Amelia," he warns, eyes dark and endless, filled with a level of obsession I never thought I'd witness. "You have to do this, or they'll get worse."

We dealt with my wounds ourselves the day Damien rescued me. Unfortunately, the burns on my feet got infected. I don't regret it. I couldn't handle being around people that day. I needed quiet. I needed him.

The nurse is kind. Gentle. She always makes sure to be careful with me. But after everything, I developed a quirk, I hate anyone but Damien touching me.

"I'll be right here," he promises. "She just needs to change the dressing."

I nod once.

A knock sounds at the door.

"Come in," he calls.

The nurse steps in with bright eyes and a calm smile.

Damien shifts, pulling me into his lap, his arms caging me.

"You two are adorable," she says. She always says that.

"Let's get this over with, sweetheart," she hums as she sets up.

I feel Damien's body tense as she kneels and unwraps the gauze on my feet. He watches her closely, never letting her touch me without me being on him. I'm grateful she respects our boundaries. She's an angel.

She works quickly, replacing the gauze and applying something cool that soothes the sting.

"I see a lot of couples," she murmurs, "but you two? You're something else." She chuckles. "It's the way he looks at you."

I glance at Damien.

His eyes are locked on my feet, his jaw tight. He still blames himself for not finding me sooner. For not being able to take me to the hospital that night without falling apart.

I don't like anyone touching me. He hates anyone else touching me. A match made in heaven…or hell.

She finishes up, securing the last bandage.

I finally breathe. "Thank you."

As soon as the door clicks shut behind her, Damien's phone buzzes in his pocket.

He turns to stone.

He pulls it out, glances at the screen, and starts to stand, carefully moving me off his lap. I react instantly, my fingers wrapping around his wrist.

No.

No secrets.

Not anymore.

I don't say it aloud. He sees it in my eyes.

He makes his choice. He answers.

"I don't know where your daughter is, Richard."

A pause. He cracks his neck.

"If you don't have a tight enough leash on her, that sounds like your problem."

I can only hear his side of the call, but I don't need more.

It's Richard. Linda's father.

"Didn't you arrange her marriage? If she ran, that's on you." His voice sharpens. Cold. Unforgiving. "This is the last time I want to hear about this. Linda is not my business. Not my concern."

I am.

Only me.

He sounds convincing. But we both know where Linda is. Somewhere in Hell, her ashes scattered with the dirt. Good riddance.

Damien told me he broke one of his long-standing rules that night: he doesn't kill women.

But Linda?

She wasn't a woman. She was evil in flesh.

Neither of us regrets it. He tells me often, if he could go back, he would've made her death slower.

His thumb draws circles on my thigh, like he needs the reminder. I'm here. In his arms. And no one will take me away.

Linda took me to my death with a smile on her face.

Guess what, Linda?

Only one of us is still standing. And it's not you, bitch.

I settle back beside Margaret, who looks too small in that bed. I have to keep reminding myself that we made it.

I squeeze her hand again.

For a long moment, nothing happens.

Then—

A faint pressure.

A weak squeeze back.

I nearly jump out of my chair.

"Damien," I call, my heart hammering in my chest. "Damien!"

"I see it," he says, eyes wide.

Margaret's lashes flutter before she pries her eyes open.

"Hey," I breathe, reaching for the cup of water on the bedside table. "Here. Drink."

She doesn't even glance at the cup. Instead, she reaches for my face, forcing me to meet her gaze.

Her voice is hoarse. "Is it true?"

"What?"

Margaret swallows hard, her throat working. "Is it over?"

I understand now. It takes a second, but I nod.

Her body sinks deeper into the mattress, like she can finally rest.

"I heard you," she murmurs.

She heard me. The stories I told her, the reassurance, the pleading. She heard all of it.

She turns her head slightly, her eyes landing on Damien. "He burned them?"

Damien pushes off the wall and steps closer. His face is unreadable. "Every single one."

Margaret chokes on a sound, a half sob, half laugh. But it's not sadness. It's relief.

She looks back at me. "We're free?"

I nod again.

Her lips part like she wants to say something, but nothing comes out.

I know what she's feeling.

What it's like to carry fear for so long, only to realize it's gone.

"We survived," she marvels.

"We did."

"Turns out the Hellkeeper was real after all." Her lips curl into something that almost resembles a smile. "But he was on our side the whole time."

I've never thought about it that way before.

Damien. The Hellkeeper.

My Hellkeeper.

Still lost in thought, I reach for the nurse call button and press it.

Those old scriptures, the myths that filled my childhood with fear, maybe they weren't myths after all. Maybe they were warnings. But the Hellkeeper, no matter what, has always been on my side.

The nurse arrives and begins fussing over Margaret. I step away and go stand beside Damien.

The news wouldn't shut up about what happened. A fire, they said. An accident that spread too fast, swallowing everything in its path. Nothing survived. And the bodies? Burned to ash.

I don't feel guilty for the people I knew my whole life. They tried to kill me, and they would've succeeded if Damien hadn't found me first.

I'm just as morally gray as he is. And I wouldn't change a thing.

The police were on me the second I returned. Questions. Suspicion. It was overwhelming.

But Damien has friends in the right places. Friends who made things easier. They fed me a story, one I had to repeat like I believed it. Damien chased the truck, which made the masked men panic and throw me out before they got caught. Simple. Believable.

No link between us and the burning village. No bodies to analyze, no bullet holes to explain. Everything was reduced to ash.

No evidence. Just a freak accident. A fire that spread too fast, too wild, leaving nothing behind. A shootout with no suspects or motive. And just like that, we walked away clean.

As soon as the nurse finishes checking on Margaret and leaves, I rush back to her.

I hesitate, but the question has been sitting heavy in my chest. Even if it's not the right time, I can't keep it in.

"Why didn't you ever tell me?"

Margaret looks at me like she's been waiting for this moment but dreading it too.

"I didn't know how," she admits. "At first, I was scared. You came from them. And for a long time, I thought maybe… maybe they sent you here to drag me back."

I shake my head. "Never."

Damien stays nearby. He never really leaves me. But he doesn't interfere.

"I know that now," she says with a deep breath. "But back then? I had to be sure. I had to protect myself. After a while, I saw too much of myself in you, Amelia.

I knew you were just like me. I didn't know how to confess that."

Why did she take the risk? Why take me in, even if she thought I might be one of them?

"But if there was even a one percent chance that you were like me, if there was even the smallest possibility that you ran away from them, I couldn't risk leaving you out in the cold. I might as well have laid next to you."

That's Margaret. A saint.

"I should've told you," she sighs.

"You don't have to feel guilty, Margaret." I try to reassure her.

She laughs weakly and brushes away a tear. "We both know that's not how guilt works."

I don't want to dwell on the past anymore.

It's behind us.

Now?

All I want to focus on is the future. One where Damien and I can finally have our happily ever after.

Chapter Twenty-Six
Amelia

Darkness lives inside me now. It grows, festers, and invades me until the only thing I know is sin and shadow. But I couldn't be happier.

It's been a month since I last stood here. A month since I returned to Hell.

Thirty days of Damien's devotion. Thirty nights of his worship. He's given me everything; more than I ever imagined I could have. I've been drowning in his love, suffocating in the way he touches me, in the way he claims me. It's been heaven.

But sometimes, we crave a little hell.

I turn, and he's there. Damien, my dark god, my executioner, my salvation. He stands before me, his eyes reflecting the ruin we left behind. Our breaths mingle in the space between us, thick with more than just desire.

We came here to play. To defile the graveyard we built.

I smile, slow and wicked, and reach for my necklace, the one he gifted me months ago. Damien once confessed he placed a tracker inside it.

"Now, that would be cheating," I murmur, holding his gaze as I wrap the chain around my fingers. I rip it straight off. The diamonds snap, and I let it fall to the dirt at my feet.

His nostrils flare, obsidian flashing behind his eyes. I see the moment he decides exactly what he's going to do to me.

I spin on my heel and run into the village.

The first few seconds are silent.

Then I hear a dark chuckle.

He gave me a head start.

The ground is uneven beneath me, dirt mixing with the ashes of those who once lived here. There's nothing left. No people. No animals. No vegetation. Just ruin. Just death. Just the memory of the village that tried to bury me; and the man who burned it to the ground.

And God, I'm wet.

The night air burns against my skin as I push forward, dodging the remains of crumbled cottages. I listen intently, waiting for the sound of his pursuit.

Nothing.

It unsettles me. Thrills me.

He's here. I know it. He's waiting. Watching.

The question is: where?

I risk a glance over my shoulder.

Nothing but darkness.

My heart pounds, adrenaline making me dizzy. I lunge forward, aiming for the shattered remnants of the place of worship ahead: the elder's shrine. Its skeletal remains stretch toward the sky like twisted fingers. If I can just—

A shadow shifts in the corner of my vision.

Too late.

I pivot hard, barely dodging his grasp. The thrill of the hunt, the chase, the inevitable capture makes me soak through my panties.

I duck behind the shrine, my chest rising and falling in uneven breaths. I peek around the edge, searching. Waiting.

Silence.

Then...a whisper of movement.

He's close.

So close.

I press a hand to my stomach, feeling the heat coiling low. I'm so turned on.

And when I move to bolt again, a hand clamps around my wrist.

I barely have time to gasp before I'm spun and shoved against the shrine. My wrists are pinned above my head, Damien's body pressing flush against mine.

I don't struggle. Instead, I tilt my head, offering my throat.

A growl rips from his chest. "You think I wouldn't find you, little flower?"

"I think you let me run longer than usual."

"I was deciding what to do with you."

"And?"

He lowers his head, teeth scraping over my jaw. "I'm going to ruin you."

And as he lifts me into his arms, carrying me through the remains of our destruction, I know I will let him.

Again.

And again.

And again.

His hands are everywhere. They feel like fire. He squeezes my ass, my breasts, my thighs. And just like every time he touches me, I feel complete.

He slams me into the cold earth, the ashes of the village sticking to my skin. His weight flattens me into the ground.

His mouth crashes onto mine. The kiss is brutal, claiming, full of the ferocity of everything he's done to this place, to these people, to me. He tastes like smoke, like blood. Like hell. Like heaven.

"I'm going to remake you. And when I'm done, you won't know where the darkness ends and you begin," he hisses, licking from my ear to my collarbone.

I bite back a moan. It's a pleasure I no longer shy from. Everything I do with Damien is right. Even in its filthiness, it's perfect.

"You were never meant for them. And you'll never be theirs again," he vows, ripping my dress down the middle. I'm left in just my wet panties. "I own you."

My body arches into his, eager. Hungry for this twisted brand of salvation.

"I've always been yours."

"You're so perfect, little flower," he whispers around a mouthful of my nipple. He tugs at it, then soothes with soft licks. I melt.

"Do you like being touched on top of what I burned for you?" he hums, mouth still wrapped around one nipple while he pinches the other.

I shudder, my body answering him before I do. Still, I nod.

He presses open-mouthed kisses on my stomach. It shines with his spit. He licks at me like an ice cream cone, and the nerves there spark straight to my clit. The pleasure is blinding.

"I will tear down empires, end legacies, burn religions for you. Say it."

"You're the only one I worship," I manage to moan.

He drags me up by my hair, forcing me onto my knees. He tugs me closer, unbuttoning his pants and pulling his cock free.

My lips part. He watches me with dark, endless hunger.

"Open wider, little sinner."

I kiss along his length, eyes wide. He pushes the tip into my mouth. I suck, swirling my tongue.

"Look at you," he murmurs. "Worshipping me like I'm the only god in your world."

I hum around him, watching his jaw clench, fingers twitching in my hair. Power rushes through me. Once, I would've been shy. Now, I love this. Love how he unravels for me. How I can make this terrifying man weak with just my lips, my hands, my body.

"Everything I destroy, I destroy for you," he rasps. "Every sin I commit, I commit for you."

He yanks me back just enough to see my face, thumb dragging over my swollen lips.

"My good girl takes me so well."

I wrap my fingers around him, stroking slow, teasing. "I can take more."

He grins before thrusting deeper. I gag, breathing through my nose to ease the pressure. My eyes water, but he holds my head still. I love it. His other hand comes up, caressing my hair as I choke on him.

"I'm the only one you'll ever bow for. The only one you'll ever need."

And he's right.

He's absolutely right.

Using my hair, he drags me away from my favorite treat. Flipping me onto my stomach, my cheek presses into the ground. My fingers claw at the dirt, digging into the remnants of what used to be. Ash clings to my skin, to him, to us. His hands drag over my back, down to my hips, and he rips my panties off. Absolutely feral.

"Feel it, Amelia. The remnants of what I burned for you. Let them look up at us. Let them witness what our religion truly is."

I can never say no to this man. My fingers curl into the soot. It gets under my fingernails, so deep I don't think I'll ever feel clean again. He watches me with dark fascination, his pupils swallowing the silver of his irises. Without warning, he thrusts inside me.

My eyes roll back from the mix of pain and pleasure, but mostly pleasure.

He pounds into me, hard and unforgiving, and I make sounds that would make the devil himself blush. Each thrust is brutal, relentless, exactly how I crave it.

"You know what you're kneeling on?" he murmurs, voice thick with possession. "Ash and dust. All that's left of the ones who hurt you. Who thought they could touch you. Look where they are now. And look where you are. Look where I've put you."

We go at it like animals. That's what Damien turns me into; an animal who can't think of anything but the pleasure he gives. I'm incoherent, unable to form words, so I let him speak.

"They burned for you," he growls. "And now, you burn for me."

We are messed up. No sane person processes trauma like we do. But this is just us. Unapologetically us. With one final thrust, he releases inside me. I follow, unraveling around him.

We collapse into each other. He pulls off his shirt and dresses me in it. We sprawl across the ground, spent and heaving.

Just as my body trembles from the aftershocks, he takes my soot-covered hand and slides something cold onto my finger. A ring. A dark metal band, a single black diamond in the center.

I stare at it, heart hammering in my chest. "You didn't even ask me to marry you."

Damien smirks. "I own you, Amelia. I don't need to ask."

It should be outrageous. But nothing has ever felt more right.

Still, I lift my chin, refusing to back down. "Then let me own you, too."

Something flickers in his eyes, raw, unguarded. Something only I get to see. He presses his forehead to mine and whispers, "You already do."

His fingers trace my jaw, keeping my gaze locked as he speaks his vows, not soft, not sweet. Dark and unbreakable.

"You are mine. In this life, in the next. In whatever hell or heaven we end up in. I vow to keep you, to claim you, to destroy anything that dares stand in our way. I will worship you with fire and ruin, Amelia. I will never let you go."

My body, my soul, every part of me is his. And I don't want it any other way.

I clutch the ring and give him my vows in return.

"I vow to never fear the dark again, because you are in it with me. I vow to love you not the way the world tells me to, but the way we were meant to. I vow to never let you kneel alone. I am yours, Damien. Yours in every way that matters."

We kiss like it's our last breath, hungry, wild, desperate to fuse into one. When we finally pull apart, tangled together on ruined earth, I let out a breathless laugh.

"Margaret and Ruby are going to be very excited."

Damien hums, kissing my ring finger, his fingers drawing lazy circles on my thighs. I smile into his chest.

Nothing in my life has ever been certain. But now?

It's him. He's my only constant.

The past is gone, burned to nothing but ash beneath our bodies. And from those ashes, something new has risen. Twisted. Unholy. Perfect.

Because love isn't just about light.

Sometimes, the most sacred love is born in the dark.

The Hellkeeper was never a myth.

The Hellkeeper is a man.

And I am his eternal sinner.

Sneak Peek

Wondering what's coming next? Here's a sneak peek into **Beautifully Deranged (Sinful Fates #1).**

Chapter One
Lola

I don't *ask* for what I want. I *take* it.

From the moment I could speak, I knew how to twist the world to my liking, how to make everything bend to my will, to my whims. And along the way, I learned to push everything and everyone away.

When I was nine, Father told me I couldn't have the toy rifle because "it's for boys." He quickly learned that no one tells me no. I screamed until his resolve cracked. Until he caved. After that, he understood that with me, it was always about *winning*. About making him see I always get what I want. He never said no again.

In high school, my painting didn't fit some mold. "Flawed," the teacher said, sneering as she told me it wouldn't be entered in the art competition. I dragged every flaw she'd buried in her own life to the surface. Every regret. Every failure. She quit the job shortly after. I just kept painting.

Then there was the nanny. She told me I couldn't have more cookies because I was getting fat. So I pointed out every flaw on her skin, every ugly mark she tried to hide with makeup. It made her squirm, and it made me smile. I ate my cookies after. Because I could. Because I always can.

Father didn't get it. He brought in therapist after therapist, thinking some label would fix me. OCD. Antisocial personality disorder. Some spectrum of autism. A bunch of fancy terms for someone who simply takes what they want. And that's what I've done. I've taken it all. I've earned it all.

And now, I want him.

Mikhail Volkov.

The bane of my existence. The only man who's ever made me feel something more than desire for things that can be bought or controlled. He's the first person who's captured my attention without even trying. That makes him dangerous.

When I told Father I wanted to move to New York to build my art career, I never expected to end up obsessing over my next-door neighbor instead.

The best thing Father ever did for me was set me up in one of the most luxurious apartments money can buy. It's where I met Mikhail. The man I've always fantasized about finally has a face, and now, it's his.

Truthfully, Father couldn't send me away fast enough. That's what happens when your personality is *too much*. People stop liking you, even the ones who are supposed to love you unconditionally.

But not Mikhail.

Not this time.

I won't push him away. Not now. Not ever. Because I know what I want, and I can become whatever he needs me to be. I'll mold myself into his perfect fantasy. The sweet girl next door. The seductive temptress. The one who won't let him go.

I watch him and I don't hide it. My eyes follow the way he moves through the building, the way he walks with that perfect, unbothered confidence. Like he owns the world.

I know everything about him.

Where he works. What time he comes and goes. How he spends his evenings, always in the gym or on long, solitary walks. The way his shirt rides up after a run, showing off those perfect abs and that delicious happy trail. I've memorized it all.

Is it stalking?

I tell myself it's not. I'm not following him. I'm just… crossing the same paths. So what if I take a walk at the exact time he leaves the building? So what if I linger near the coffee shop, hoping to see him across the street, knowing when his car pulls up? I'm not stalking. I'm just breathing the same air, standing in the same space.

Is that really so wrong?

He's gone most days. Comes back at exactly six thirty in the evening like clockwork. But sometimes, he disappears for days. Business trips? Maybe.

But when he's gone, the silence in the building feels different. Empty. Too quiet.

I tell myself it's fine. He's busy. He's important. Running a leading construction company can't be easy. But then the thought creeps in.

What if he's with someone else? A girlfriend?

I imagine him smiling with her, touching her, doing everything he doesn't do with me. I hate it. I hate it so much I feel it in my teeth.

I pray he's not. Because if he is, I want no part of it. I'm not a homewrecker; that's my line in the sand.

Watching Father cheat on my mother while she battled cancer—then watching it all come crashing down on him and his mistress—was enough proof that karma is real. And I don't play with karma.

His mistress was found murdered in a ditch. To this day, no one knows who did it. And as for him? He was diagnosed with cancer a few months after her death. It was a rough battle, but he survived.

Guess karma went a little easy on him.

The clock strikes five, snapping me out of my thoughts.

It's a ritual now. We've been doing this dance for days, and I've perfected the waiting, the anticipation.

The shower is scalding. I shave, pluck, and smooth out every little detail. Every inch of me must be perfect. After drying off, I get ready. I twist my long ginger hair into a braid, swipe on some makeup, and slip into a white bodycon dress that hugs every curve.

His presence hits like a pulse, heavy, masculine, and I instantly know he's here. I wait until it's seven, then knock.

He opens the door, and there he is.

My obsession. My silent craving.

"Hi," I say, flashing a bright, sweet smile with just the right touch of innocence.

He grumbles a hello. His voice is deep, rough. I fucking love it. He's like a bear, big, gruff, all muscle and testosterone. And I don't say "bear" lightly. He's easily six foot five. His biceps are the size of my thighs; and I've got a lot of flesh on these thighs. He's everything a man should be. Perfect.

"May I please have some sugar?" I ask, my voice sticky-sweet as I toss my hair over my shoulder, just enough to show off a little more cleavage. "I ran out. I wanted to bake something sweet."

He doesn't smile or say a word. Just turns around and grabs the sugar, handing it to me without meeting my gaze.

If he's ever wondered why I show up so dressed up every time I ask for something, he never says. I take the jug, letting my fingers brush against his. A tiny thrill runs through me.

"Thank you," I murmur. "I'll give you some cookies when I'm done."

I wait. Hoping for an invitation inside. But, as usual, he gives me a curt nod and closes the door.

I walk away, lips pouting. But just as I reach my apartment, his voice stops me.

"Lola."

My legs weaken. That's my name. On his lips. My heart skips a beat, thudding loud in my chest. Is this it? Is he finally going to ask me in?

"It seems like you need to hit the grocery store," he mutters, before slamming the door shut again.

My jaw drops.

What the fuck?

All I asked for over the past few days were some eggs, milk, and sugar. Is that really so much? God, if he ever bothered to actually *talk* to his neighbor, maybe he wouldn't have to deal with this every damn time.

I think I might just lose it.

I never actually needed any of those things. It was always just an excuse to see him. To feel that rush, that tiny moment of connection.

But every time, I end up with nothing.

Not for long.

Thank you so much for picking up my debut novella. I really hope you enjoyed the story and the characters as much as I enjoyed writing them. I can't wait to share more with you in the future!

Where to Find Me?

For updates and more about my books, please visit the following platforms:

Tiktok: @darkquickreads / @darkromanceshelf1
Instagram: @darkromanticreads
YouTube: @darkromanticreads

Until Next Time, Darling.

Printed in Great Britain
by Amazon